# THE SEVENTH ELEPHANT

Alexis Stamatis was born in Athens. He studied
Architecture at the National Technical University of
Athens and took postgraduate degrees in Architecture
and Cinematography in London. He has published four
books of poetry. His second book, *The Architecture of
Interior Spaces*, was awarded the Nikiforos Vrettakos
Poetry Prize by the Municipality of Athens in 1994.
He has worked as an architect and, more recently, as a
journalist specializing in arts and cultural issues. He is a
member of the Praxis Theatrical Society, for which he
organizes an annual programme of literary events.
*The Seventh Elephant* is his first novel.

# THE SEVENTH ELEPHANT

## Alexis Stamatis

Translated by David Connolly

A

ARCADIA BOOKS

LONDON

Arcadia Books Ltd
139 Highlever Road
London W10 6PH

www.arcadiabooks.co.uk

First published in Greece by Kedros 1998
First published in the United Kingdom by Arcadia Books Ltd 2000
Copyright © Alexis Stamatis 1998
English translation copyright © David Connolly 2000

ISBN 978-1-900-85021-6

Printed and bound by CPI Group (UK) Ltd, Croydon, CR0 4YY

The author and publishers would like to acknowledge:
J. M. Barrie, *Peter Pan* (1904) Wordsworth Editions, 1993
Stephané Mallarmé, 'Brise Marine' in P. Mansell Jones (ed.),
*The Oxford Book of French Verse*, (Oxford, 1968)
Samual Taylor Coleridge, letter to Mary Morgan, in E. L. Griggs (ed.),
*Letters of Samuel Taylor Coleridge*, (Oxford, 1959), vol. 3

Arcadia Books Supports English PEN *www.englishpen.org* and
The Book Trade Charity *http://booktradecharity.wordpress.com*

*Arcadia Books distribution are as follows:*

*in the UK and elsewhere in Europe:*
Macmillan Distribution Ltd
Brunel Road
Houndmills
Basingstoke
Hants RG21 6XS

*in the USA and Canada:*
Dufour Editions
PO Box 7
Chester Springs
PA19425

*in Australia/New Zealand:*
NewSouth Books
University of New South Wales
Sydney NSW 2052

To my father

*The gods are just, and of our pleasant vices make instruments to scourge us*

William Shakespeare, *King Lear*

# Contents

WHEN HE'D READ THE LETTER, he folded it and put it in the file on his desk together with all the others. Three matches were lying beside the ink-pot. He picked up two of them and joined their ends, so making a shape like a pyramid. He got up from his chair and stared at it. He didn't like it. He thought it oppressive, as if it were hemming him in. He took the third match and placed it parallel to the notional floor in the middle of the pyramid. The result, a capital 'A', was more to his satisfaction. Then he took it apart and set about another arrangement. He placed the one match above the other in parallel. He looked at them again. He didn't like the co-ordination, the parallelism. He took the third match and used it to join the left end of the bottom match with the right end of the upper one. The shape was complete. A 'Z', completely geometrical, took shape before him. Two shapes with three matches. The same components, a different result. His attention turned to the third match, the diagonal one, it seemed somehow different from the others. He took it, struck it, let it burn and then he understood. It was this third match that prevented any boxing, that joined the nonconvergent, that led the way to the blazing end, leaving behind two lines that would never meet.

# Aura

Midday on deck, the sun directly overhead, and sea, everywhere sea, sea and gulls, all azure and white. In his head he could feel those tiny tails as Mitya, one of the three Russian brothers, referred to them. They were trembling, that's exactly how it was; there are these tiny tails that tremble and then remember, this is what's bothering him. This very attribute, that makes them vibrate, tremble and then remember, unnerves him. How he wished that those tails didn't exist, that he could see and think at the same time, that the image and its processing might be one single procedure. What a waste of time for the image to enter the tail, to stir it and then for this to call up memory, to inform and compare,

3

to process and decide! Of course the worst thing about all this business is that he eventually remembers. And it was this that he was trying consciously, but also out of an instinct for self-preservation, to play down. As much as he could.

He stretches his legs. A twinge of pain in the knee. Ever sensitive in the joints, an indeterminable pain, vague. The sun scorching. He feels sleepy. He's tired, exhausted. There's a kind of exhaustion that's the worst of all: trying not to think of anything. Like now. He wants to empty himself. Of thoughts, of images. Impossible. A bee is circling round him. He wafts it away. It comes back. Goes away again. Somewhere to the south she'll be thinking of him with a wet towel over her face. Her legs sunk deep in the sand. Even deeper. He'd recognized the telephone call straight away. She put down the phone in less than five seconds, but the breath of the long-distance call had given her away. The silent reminder. The worst nightmare. He stretches out his legs still more. A slight pain in the coccyx. Useless in any case. Remnant of a tail. The animal disappears from upon us. Only a few vestiges remain. Some nooks to remind us of it.

He looks at his watch. 4:44 p.m., 4.9.95. Fours again. Like nails in the briny afternoon. A

light, refreshing breeze is blowing. I'm travelling, he thinks.

## 2.

'Allez-vous à Paros?' from the chair next to him.

An engaging, well-built young man, with
broad shoulders and hawkish profile, from
Paris, a medical student. He was obviously in a
mood for conversation – or rather for a mono-
logue. In a characteristically nasal voice, he tells
him that it's the second time he's going to the
island. On hearing the name Paris, he again
sees before him rue Daguerre with its market-
place, the cooked meats and the seafood, with
the thousands of colours and with the sense of
festivity streaming from every stall. At the same
time, he also sees Les Halles and the houses he
frequented and the environment of the *enfants
gâtés* of the French capital with whom he had
shared – by chance? by choice? – a crucial period in his life. And of course the salon with the
exhibition of antique furniture, as he would
later admit with sarcasm. Next, a film came into
his mind: *La Haine*. Particularly the final scene.
With the shots a sound track on the face of
Said, the Arab, the Foreigner. Then, with the
associations coming thick and fast, he journeyed

in his mind to the Emirates, to the warm sea, to his meeting with Otaiba, to the meal in kaftans, to the souk, to the hotel, to the bottles bought illegally at five times the normal price...

Jacques Delamarche went on for an hour. He talked about his studies, his separation, about St Germain, about Mittérrand's illegitimate daughter. Then he got fed up. He was like a child clumsily playing with a toy for some time before tiring of it: a toy that in any case was only following as a matter of form – as his mind was on other things – he went to the toilet leaving Jacques on his own smoking his last cigarette. Once there he took out the small bottle and took four large swigs. He gazed at himself in the mirror and smiled at his swollen eyes.

3.

The sun bright, a mitrailleuse mercilessly shooting out its rays. Below, a hissing rose from the amorphous, glowering face of the sea. In the distance, a faint grey, the island appears like an illusion. On a wooden form beside the boats a middle-aged couple are talking. He listens.

'Do you remember last year how lovely it was?'

'Yes, but not like in 1980. An orgasm of building, that's what it is.'

'And the people are so different...'

'That's people for you. They change.'

'People change along with the houses.'

'This island's got something, a magnetism. It forms a triangle with Delos and Santorini. Isosceles.'

'You're right about that. It's certainly got something.'

'A magnetism.'

He feels a certain lethargy. A lethargy caused by the sun, that makes him think of other suns. A condensed light hurls wet pointed darts. He shudders. He puts on his earphones: Jonathan Richman, 'That Summer Feeling'. Two more swigs. The air is shining like a gold ring at midday. A hydrogen molecule from the alcohol vanishes into his guts. The spirit is transformed into acetone. Everything alters, everything changes. And he, sad for some time now, doesn't know. He doesn't know that what he feels right now, what for so many years has been inexplicably causing him pain, that same thing is here now. It's here and travelling. With him.

## 4.

Before long he'll set foot on the island. He doesn't know if that pang he feels is due to the recollection, the return and expected comparison, or if it's fear, the fear that's waiting to be confirmed, that seizes little rasping breaths from his lungs and merges them into a pronounced difficulty in breathing; or perhaps it's that expectation, responsible for those tiny sharp twinges, that pushes him to forcefully join with, to clutch at, to desperately hang onto the future blowing before him like a foreign breeze. A cool breeze, that spreads all around with a deceptive charm and leads him, with a waning moon, to a wager, to a throw of the dice whose significance he's not yet aware of. The dice roll and on the edge of the cube the numbers whirl round – the numbers, the coincidences and correspondences that once again accompany him to this place which, as he'd just heard them put it very aptly, has a magnetism, a kind of radiance that imbues the darkness spreading over the harbour with an otherworldly sheen, just like a cloud of electrical fields that struggle and open this adjacent, this interim life of his like a fan. A life that resembles breathing which becomes regular only with difficulty, with the guts churning round, the senses inert, with a tongue that wants to say something but can't.

He's come to the island after two years of
voluntary confinement at home. Two years with
virtually no work – the fault of the cheques that
kept arriving from the 1990 contract – the pros
and cons of being self-employed. Two years on
the threshold of memory, whole months erased,
others vague, with events fragmented and very
few moments of clarity, such as all that had
happened in the last month, with the continual
arguments, the final straw and the unavoidable
end. Now he really is alone, without a house to
hide in, without a woman, without an alibi. Just
him and the outside world, and that scares him.
He feels that between him and the environment
there exists a huge natural problem, a problem
of organic dimensions, and that all he can do –
and with great effort – is to allay it, forget it.

He has no plan. No. There's no programmed
sequence of action, he has no course mapped
out. Everything will come of its own accord, he
won't force anything. It's clear to him now that
he's not the one to decide. What decides is the
eye of a pachyderm that he's swallowed. An eye
that, firmly lodged in his guts, will observe him,
supervise him, spy on him for ever. For the
time being he still feels himself hiding in a peculiar flora, in a green swamp with walls of
horn to the right and left. Every now and then,
he sees a gigantic shadow approaching. Then he

reaches out his arms and stretches as far as he can. As far as he can to touch the shadow, to bite the darkness, to enter into the liberating shade.

The gangway is lowered. Small lights shine. He feels as if he's flying. Towards the lights. That go out. He sets foot on the island wrapped in the soft sound of the rippling sea. He notices the regularities of the constructed shapes, the thousands of glittering lights, and beneath the dimmed stars of the summer night he feels his life suspended between the damp air and the sad earth he's treading on.

# Bacillus

## 5.

'Alone this year? Where's...'

'Alone, Mrs Vasso. Alone.'

'Why's that, dear boy? What d'you get up to over there? How d'you live like that? The stress'll be the end of you all.'

'It's not the stress.'

'All right, all right. Come on, come on in. I've kept you the same room as you had the year before last. With the balcony over the harbour.'

'What about the light? It wakes me up with the dawn.'

Presently, lying on the bed, he gazes at the windows covered with grey paper and insulating tape. He feels like a protozoon in a test-tube. He feels excessively tiny, confined, like a fungus, like a deadly virus that has to be isolated in a container, in a box. An isolated box. His room. Some people's rooms are always like that. And their lives too. Though in Mrs Vasso's house, the ground is prone to leakages. The girl from Sweden – the first smiles had already been exchanged – the couple from Italy, the lad from Thessaloniki, the Dutch surfer. Five young people. The shared bathroom clean. An opportunity for conversation.

He fell asleep and dreamed of a woman who fell in love with someone, but who couldn't savour her love because she didn't know how, she'd never learned how to love and be loved. First she was giving and longed for him, then she held it all back and deflated him, till eventually she didn't know who she was. She felt herself divided and went crazy and had to be taken off, like at the end of *A Streetcar Named Desire*. He woke in a sweat at around nine. He was never one to rely on the kindness of others. Even less so of strangers. He didn't know the woman, he thought, and dressed with ungainly movements, knocking over the plastic cup with the drink. The Absolut spilled onto the floor. Cursing, he went over to the fridge. He's fighting. It's not easy to fight against your own soul. It's an unequal contest. Like all forms of civil strife.

# 6.

Lina. Now blonde with highlights. She's put on a few pounds, he tells her, not without some wish to vex her. She brushes it off with her familiar cackling laughter. Unconcerned about anything. That's how she always was, in whatever situation arose in her life. In her marriage, in her divorce. In every emotional matter, the self-preservation mechanism worked overtime. In the past, she'd been an actress and played in avant-garde performances immediately after the fall of the junta. Later, she became involved with Hadjidakis's attempts at a free radio, then she began designing jewellery. Now they're sitting together in a small bar at the centre of a little seaside village which, for some strange reason, bears the name of a city in the north, one street above the cafés, in a narrow lane, so narrow that the balconies on either side are only a few feet from each other. The bar is small, neat and tidy, with two blue iron tables outside on the paved road. At one of these he is sitting with Lina, the owner. At the other is an eighty-year-old guy, good-looking with sea-blue eyes, a former chairman of the local community, together with a girl.

He: a white shirt with silver buttons, black jeans, white trainers, freshly-shaven; the Absolut in front of him. Now with orange. She: a black blouse, skin-tight trousers, brown hair, grey-green eyes and large eyebrows that appear to have served as a refuge for any number of black images. It was about twelve-thirty when with a sudden levity their gazes crossed the artificial lighting to come together, searchingly and embarrassingly, in a notional straight line. And they both felt an unexpected force. It was like an instantaneous perception of the Other, a momentary biopsy of his image. Through Lina, who knew them, he invited them over to his table. The introductions were made politely and with a formality unsuited to the circumstances. Her name was Z. He bought her a drink, lit her cigarette. He knew how to conduct himself.

## 7.

Music at full blast with staccato sounds; it shakes the walls which for the most part are bare and only small corners with decorations of fish bones solid and permanent relics incompatible with the rhythm and the sound a whirl a mixture of East and West spreading over her body and she swaying sensuously and forgetting in her red mind where she is also forgetting T. their seven-year relationship and the island and travelling with headlights that change from blue to yellow on the highways camping on the roadside alone on the dance floor and everyone looking at her and desiring her and Central Europe shamelessly letting itself go in her at four o'clock in the morning on a Greek island.

He is holding a handful of jasmine; he puts it in his shirt to dry. Within him, in contrast to the loud repetitive sound, he sings a tuneful song. It's a sad song, sweet like her. He gazes at her. Just like all the others.

# 8.

They left the club at around six. As they were walking hand in hand down by the tiny harbour, he leaned over and kissed her. She responded straight away. He tried to isolate the feeling that had been following him all through the evening – something like the side-effect following a large inoculation – and to concentrate on the half-open mouth, on the misty grey-green eyes. He almost said something but reflected that he wouldn't be the one who was speaking. Almost trembling, he began to think of the slovenliness, the irregularities, the failure. Suddenly, she pursed her lips in such a way as if to say: 'Yes,

I understand, it doesn't matter, it happens to everyone.' Then he made a wise choice. He allowed the spirits and his spirit to be reconciled, he ordered a truce between the warring cells, he declared his state to be a special interim regime and decided to spend the rest of the night – what night? – in that artificial moratorium, in that peculiar alliance.

'I like travelling, it's the only way to live on this earth,' she said to him. He answered 'Yes' with a nod of agreement, and they headed towards his small room.

# Chrysalis

## 9.

How ridiculous it would be to try to find the
origin of your name travelling backwards up the
river to its source and to hope to discover up
there, hooked on a low branch, damp, a piece of
paper with your name, that which makes you
what you are, and for you to be here with her at
nine in the morning, awake, in a double bed
that takes up the whole room, with sheets of
paper over the windows to keep out the rays of
light, and the two bodies, unknown to each
other a few hours ago, coming together, approaching each other with a natural sluggish-
ness, and for each of them, reaching out, to feel
the turning of the body opposite; and a light-
ness raising the long thighs, the sculptured

mouth opening the curved loins and the panting breeze enfolding them round him together
with the perspiration. For them to meet for the
first time, to be bound by a common rope, for
each to pull the other deep into the labyrinth of
his inner mind and then for a current of refreshing liquid to branch out, unite and relieve.
Then, for the one to gaze at the landscape of the
other where he'd received hospitality and to recognize the river that he has just travelled
down, with its brown banks, its secret eddies
and the insects' new-born buzzing, and for him
to see his name large, deep, enormous on the
river-bed, carved on the stones. His very own
name, from which some other hand, in some
other latitude, has stripped the initial, a huge,
yellowed 'A', in order to throw it, useless insulating tape, into the fathomless depths of the
same southern sea.

He opened his eyes. He felt hot. It was noon.
He reached out to hold her. She'd gone.

## IO.

In the boat heading towards the tiny beach with
a dozen or so fair-haired kids from Central
Europe. She's from Central Europe too. Yet so

different! Unclassifiable. He takes the withered jasmine from his pocket. He plucks a leaf from it. To protect him from evil. The beach appears in the distance. Small, virtually empty, deep blue water, not a trace of shade. He'd remain there for four hours, in the sun, reading and swimming. The sun would provide him with that pleasant daze, aided that is by the Absolut which had been carefully packed in the bag together with the books. He'd read and the words would be instantaneously transformed into images, hot images, burning together with his face and body, scorching so you could no longer keep hold of them. And then he would plunge into the sea, into the sea that he so adores, and he'd dig in the sand so the images would be buried, so the ground would swell with words.

The boat pulls into the shore. He stands up straight, dressed in black, with sunglasses. The Dutch girl gives him a sidelong look, showing signs of interest. He's not even aware of it. He smiles. He smiles to himself because he knows. There's another foreign girl who's more than interested.

## II.

The next day. He wakes with a heavy head full of dreams.

He's in a huge bed with a pile of sheets all twisted up together. He tries to free himself, but it's impossible. Linen and limbs have become one. He remains there like that, swathed, unable to move, looking through the window at the shadow of a tree spread gigantically over the wall opposite. Gathered in the neighbouring field are eleven female workers with garlands of flowers in their hair and the same number of grimy men drinking from cups full of red liquid – maybe wine, maybe blood. Beside him is a young woman in an armchair on wheels, with colourless eyes and a white face. Her name begins with 'L'. She was once to be his wife.

He gets ready to go to the same beach. Halfway down the steps, he bumps into her. If she'd come two minutes later, they would have missed each other. A little later, sitting astride a rented scooter, he hugs her from behind. The lovely landscape passes before him and he sees the back of her ear, her windswept hair, the tip of her breast. He gives in to her whim to drive. On the beach, naked as she is, she says to him with coquetry mixed with modesty: 'I hope you're not offended.' He is certainly not.

## 12.

At midday, she invited him to go and eat together with friends of hers. Francis and Gwen, middle-aged Americans, had been living on the island for some twelve years. In October, they'd leave for America for three years 'to take in some Atlantic air', as they put it. He was a university lecturer and she was a writer, together they made a colourful, *sui generis* couple. He wondered what she could have in common with these people as he observed her absorbed and ecstatic listening about karmic auras, horoscopes, Buddhism, Zen and the occult. And all this intermingled with a pragmatic philosophy, with plans for making money, company references, intangible deeds and bonds, and he felt – what irony, he of all people! – that he must protect her, open her eyes, explain to her that this was not the right path, that, yes, it was only right to question one's existence, but let's not be taken in so easily, there are plenty of frauds ready to exploit our natural curiosity and all the rest.

In the evening, a stroll round the tiny harbour. 'Every organ in the body represents a feeling,' she told him. 'Problems with the kidneys means criticism, disappointment; problems with the stomach means fear of what's new.' 'And with the liver?' he asks. 'The liver is the seat of anger and the primitive emotions. Problems with the liver means a dejected person, one trying to deceive himself.'

That night at the taverna.

'Look at that rock,' he says to her. 'Doesn't it look like a small elephant?'

'I've never seen an elephant close up,' she answers surprisingly annoyed.

# Diptych

## 13.

In the afternoon, she returned to her hotel. It was their last night on the island. That was it. He had planned to stay three days, to temporarily clear his mind of the previous month together with everything that had mounted up, to plunge head-first into new things, surrounded in another light, and at least for a while to live a life that appeared normal, to begin to behave in keeping with whatever stimulated him, to keep to some basic rhythm, some kind of regularity, however primitive this may be.

From as far back as he can remember himself, he'd had some problem with reality. He experienced the present as a diptych: on the outside was the truth of the world and on the inside was his own truth, an exclusive truth, *the inner seam of a suit*. He was in negotiation with his surroundings at every moment, at every moment of his life, starting from what he knew from the time he'd begun to be aware, and from before of course, from the time he was deep inside, because there too he learned how to store things away. His life inside the narrow sack was a continual learning process, until he emerged and entered another, larger sack, with more storage room, with a darker colour, and – the main thing – a sack that he had to share with others right to the end. But this storing away is by its very nature unconscious – how is he to distinguish what he thinks he's learned consciously on his own from what's already been written within him as knowledge and which prevents him from understanding that his present actions are exceedingly logical, are above all necessary! But no, he's curious, he wants to explain and analyse every little thing, wants to record it in his mind's indispensable writing so that he might be at every moment and at all times informed and ready for every eventuality. Which is why now, at the hotel, he goes to the toilet and takes the bottle out of the bag. He drinks so as not to remember, so as to temporarily disconnect the internal sorting machine that automatically classifies and processes. He drinks so as to deceive those tiny tails and destroy the memory of that night, the night that he'll face the cause of all this incoherence imprinted on the body of the Other, as well as on his own. Unfortunately in the morning he won't remember. Yet.

# 14.

The last day. Breakfast in the harbour. An omelette for both of them and hot coffee. He pays for her. She's grateful. She's sorry she has to leave. She draws him a plan of how to find her at the airport in three days' time when she comes to Athens in order to leave for Europe – what organization, Central European upbringing! he thinks to himself and keeps the piece of paper as a souvenir. She'll have a two-hour wait between flights. He promises her that he'll be there. He won't go though. He'll be too scared.

When it's time for her to leave, he accompanies her to the boat clutching the plan in his fist. He watches her sunburned back disappear as the gangway closes. In returning, he's left behind him two joys. The one from the previous day, his own, he left in his room carefully folded to smell that dried jasmine, because it's that kind of joy that he didn't know how to negotiate,

because he didn't know where it came from –
he couldn't know, nor did the tiny tails inform
him, nor anything – and the other, her joy, he
simply ignored, because he was still in no position to understand what joys and people together mean.

## 15.

The first letter.

*Dearest,*
*Thanks for the wonderful moments, the sharing,*
*the understanding, the identifying, the conversation,*
*the dancing, the bars, the beach and the bed, it was*
*all wonderful. I feel you very close to me. I miss*
*you.*

Z.

He hides the letter in his most secret drawer.
As if embarrassed. He buries it deep beneath
other papers that he doesn't look at any more.
In a while, this too will be forgotten, he reflects.
Perhaps years later someone will find it.
Perhaps. Now he has to hide it. Because danger
is close by. Very close by.

# 16.

He spent almost two weeks shut up in his home. He went out maybe two or three times, the cinema, family obligations, friends. For his family, he put on a mask. He tried to appear dignified, constraining his inner turmoil as much as he could. He'd lost touch with most of his friends; his behaviour over the past four or five years was too erratic, too unconventional for them. They'd most likely written him off by now, and the truth is that they'd already put up with a great deal – in fact, some of them tried to make him open his eyes, why have you let yourself get like that, why are you ruining your life, where's your old self, and such like. Naturally, he wouldn't accept any of this, nor did he really understand what they meant. Resigned to whatever fate brought, he let time flow by, hoping for what he glibly called *'justice from within'*, an intuition, a presentiment, that in the past had saved him from numerous pitfalls. It seems though that even that store of metaphysical medicine had been used up as, for some time now, things had been sinking deeper and deeper. He could clearly see the two sides to himself, the one, with which he'd grown up, wrapped inside the other, the adult one, that was stifling him, like an airtight wrapping, preventing him from breathing.

He thought of her very often. He thought of a number of random things that she'd told him about the bad treatment she'd been subjected to as a child, about her mother who beat her, who chased her with scissors and bicycle pumps, who left her hungry for days, who called her a whore and a mental retard. He remembered her telling him how it is to have grown up with a psychologically sick mother, how it is never to feel calm and secure. In her last letter, she told him that she'd saved up some money and that she could come for a while to Athens, if, of course, that's what he wanted. He'd answered her affirmatively, that he wanted it very much, that he was anxious to see her. And it really was anxiety that he felt.

# Elephant

## 17.

In the large, sunny room he engages in conversation with Mr Georgiades in a friendlier atmosphere than he had expected. It was just sixteen hours before that he'd made the decision to see him. Now he was here, face to face. On the wall behind him an air-conditioner and an engraving by the renowned Sikeliotis depicting some scene or other from the Resistance.

They agreed on the general plan. He would accept him. On certain conditions, of course. The visit would have to be paid for even if he didn't go, unless there was an immediate need for hospitalization. Twice a week to begin with, perhaps three times later. They would need

29

maybe three years. He was away on holiday from 15 July to 30 August, two weeks at Easter and two at Christmas. In other words, nine and a half working months. He could ask him anything he wanted, though Mr Georgiades reserved the right not to answer immediately but to return to the matter at some later meeting. On closing the door, he found himself in a cold corridor. A door opened at the end of the corridor and, before it closed again, he had time to see a look of curiosity clearly printed on the face of an elderly woman.

He took the lift. He felt as if he were running over a dead animal in his car. The animal's eyes were blood red and wide-open and he could see himself in them. It was an animal with a thick hide, grey skin and a long tapering end in front like a tail. A microscopic elephant, a miniature pachyderm. Suddenly, he heard the sound of ropes and metals creaking. For a moment he was scared, then he realized that it was the lift. It was an old apartment block. Before coming out of the cubicle, he had first to open the inner door. Outside, in the fresh air, the first thing that came into his mind was that she was arriving from Europe that same evening. He'd tell her everything.

# 18.

How could he let his eyes fill with tears and allow these to drop on the table-cloth and with all those people around? How could he do it, let himself go like that in front of all those people who were looking askance at him from the other tables while he went on crying and explaining to her ... There's a limit, coming after a long process, full of guilt and remorse, after which a person decides to drop the pretence and permits anything, making use in all its splendour of a most charming alibi: the truth. So now, after half a bottle of Absolut at home and a bottle of wine in the taverna in Mavromichalis Street, it's the truth that leads him to construct an explanation, one that's honest and complete. Yes, he feels an urgency to state the facts, which he narrates in detail. But the description and the reality become confused when it comes to the evaluation, to the sorting out, to the *underlying cause*.

How relaxing though to be a guest in your own truth, to enjoy it with someone else, to allow the other person to feel it, to share it! There are times when truth too needs to be wrapped up in a warm blanket in the arms of its partner and to lie there all night before a burning fireplace.

She didn't say a word. Every so often she nodded her head, came out once or twice with 'I understand', and when he finished, she took him by the hand and they headed home. Once there she told him her story.

They spent a week together in Athens. The time passed pleasantly for both of them. A few drops of sweat that they left at night on the pillow had dried by morning. All that remained was a grey stain that puzzled her.

## 19.

She was born in a village in Bavaria. Her father was German and taught Cosmography and Mathematics at the University of Munich. A man of diverse talents, he was also a very respectable painter and an even better poet. Extensive extracts from his collection *Episode from the Deep*, containing short poems and Haiku, were included in the *Anthology of Modern German Poetry*, published by Jovis.

Her mother was English and in her youth had been crowned Miss Belsize Park; later she'd worked as a model and before meeting her father, had been involved in the pop culture of the pre-Beatles era. It's said that she was a close friend of Cliff Richard and had taken part in the vocals on the record 'Please Don't Tease', released in 1960. She'd met her father on a tour to Germany and they married two months later. They had two children, she and her sister Bessie, who was one year younger. The family settled in London and the children attended well-known public schools. She was always top of the class, the best and most popular pupil. On the contrary, her younger sister was a very average student and much less pretty. In 1968, when she was six years old, her parents got divorced and the girls remained in England with their mother. Their father returned to Germany with his lover, whom he later married, and today he is a local official in a small town of one thousand inhabitants just outside Munich. Their mother suffered a serious nervous breakdown and for many years now has been under close psychiatric observation, suffering as she does from a persecution complex and often having fits of hysteria.

When she finished school, she began to travel. She visited many countries: Canada, Spain, Sweden, India and for the last five years she has been coming every summer to Greece. She always has a suitcase in her hands. To earn a living she gives English lessons, edits texts for a publishing company and writes travel features for a woman's magazine in London. For the last three years she has been living in Munich. She's just getting over a long-standing relationship with a man nineteen years older than her, who is a top executive in German Television. She is a Sagittarian and believes she's lived at least six previous lives. Her favourite book is *The Celestine Prophecy*.

## 20.

*My dearest,*

*I'm thinking of you and can't wait to see you in my home town, as we agreed, and next year, of course, to be living together in Athens. It's amazing how so much has happened so soon, in the space of a few days. And yet it seems so right. A combination of the right circumstances and a deep bonding, and both of us changing direction in life. I was really moved by what you said to me in Athens. I sensed something in common: we both live a hectic life, with lots of people around us, yet in reality, we're both alone, we're loners, and it seems we like it. Me, for instance, I'm deep in myself at the moment, I feel distant in spite of all the extroversion I've shown recently. It seems that Greece brings out my good side. Back here though lots of fears have cropped up again, together with bad health, indecisiveness and a fair amount of tears. There's no doubt that it's an important time. The lull before the storm. Or the storm before the lull. We'll see.*

*I miss you.*

Z.

What is it that she's trying to say to him? She's writing about time, circumstance. Here, he can hardly even arrange his own time. His own time doesn't conform to any discernible sequence, his time is a long thread completely frayed, an interminable tangle, and the only thing interrupting the continuity are some knots that intervene, some knots that form a juncture in the course of his history and, in the lump that they create, imprison both the before and the after. His present is precisely these knots.

# First photograph

'I met him on the island. He's strange, but at times very open and generous with me, with his time, at others close to himself, tight-lipped, shut up inside his own world. Sometimes he scares me, at others I feel more at ease with him than I've ever felt with anyone, and I like it a lot. I like it that he writes to me. I write to him quite a lot too. We play a game with photos. He told me that every month he'll send me a photo of himself with a five-year gap.'

'He looks very young in this one,' Bessie said with a hint of disapproval in her voice.

'Yes, he's sixteen.'

'He seems embarrassed, his posture ... And

his smile ... reserved, as if he wants to hide something. His eyes half-closed; he seems bothered by the sun.'

'He's short-sighted. He didn't wear contact lenses then, you can tell.'

'And that blue shirt buttoned up to the neck ... He seems as if he's choking.'

'He's obviously got himself ready to pose. He must be on the balcony of an apartment block, you can see other blocks in the background.'

'A sweet, frightened kid.'

'A confused, nervous adolescent.'

'He doesn't look to me particularly dangerous, sis.'

'I don't know, I'm confused too. After Tony, I'm especially cautious.'

'Have you told mum?'

'She doesn't listen to me any more. Only when she takes her pills and then her mind's elsewhere.'

'Better she doesn't know. I don't tell her anything any more, I can't stand the hysteria.'

'Samuelson called by again yesterday. He thinks she should be in a clinic. The other night she slept at the police station, she was afraid they'd come and rob her again.'

'Don't give me all the details. I've had all I can of that hysteria.'

'Of course, you never had to face the full storm. Anyway.'

'Let's not go into all that. Here, put it back in the album.'

'He's coming in two weeks.'

'To London?'

'No, to Munich. I'm leaving next Tuesday, I've got things to do.'

'Do you love him?'

'I don't know, I've started to say it to him, but I honestly don't know what it means to tell someone that you love him.'

'What it means? It's just a word. Or rather three words. You feel that the other moves you, fascinates you and you tell him so: I love you.'

'But if you feel it, why do you have to say it?'

# Fantasies

## 21.

He tidies up his notes, something he does only
rarely – he's obliged to do it only when his
drawers become full of all sorts of notebooks,
papers, cards. Inside he finds stray thoughts,
impressions from events that were recorded at
their inception, ideas, plans that were never carried out, unsent letters. He stops at a torn note
written, so it seems, on the computer. A year
before. He goes over to his desk and opens the
file. He reads:

*I don't know what memory is if not one more
faculty of mind. Yes, I'm left in total confusion by
uttering a sentence where I have to put the verb in
the past tense. But isn't it necessary for the smooth*

*running of our organism? Doesn't it feed us like a continual fuel supply? Don't we live in order to continually fill in this huge papyrus, so that our Being won't collapse tomorrow like a house of cards, when all hope has been lost and the sails of the voyage are floating broken on the surface of the sea? Memory, memory that transgresses, butchers, reviving the very same precious, ultimate value: that which existed.*

He gets up and shuts off the computer. The files sink into their digital sleep. A white dot of concentrated memory remains on the screen. He turns off the light. The dot remains there staring at him.

## 22.

He's not afraid of planes. He's not afraid of the flight. He's afraid of what's new. As with every-thing new, he first has to introduce himself. He says to himself: so, this morning I'm leaving for Europe, in five or six hours I'll be ringing her bell, I'll say to her: 'Look, I'm here, I'm here for you,' I'll smile and I'll take her in my arms and we'll go to bed. A wreck now from almost daybreak, sleepless all night from the worry, he waits for his flight. He's never been to that city before nor even to that country. What a way life turns out! Now he ought to be lying down, calm (?) and reading the morning newspapers. Yet here he was, at the airport, with a black travel bag packed with all the necessities: Absolut, newspapers, magazines, with him sleepless, ready for a new five-day adventure. The excuse appears convincing: a new, unknown country, a new, promising relationship.

At the airport. Non-smoking. Window. Seat 22A. He's wearing a black silk shirt, grey trousers, black boots. The plane is air-conditioned. There's a strange coolness, almost plastic. Sitting beside him is a middle-aged woman with a turquoise dress and a beret with flowers. Extremely likeable. After the demonstration on the use of the life-jacket, she turns to him and, in a voice surprisingly soft for a German woman, asks 'Is this your first time?' and smiles at him. He immediately blushes as if ashamed of his own existence, of his clothes, of his sleeplessness, of the drinks he's had, of his blood that's thickening. He wishes he were elsewhere, far away, alone with himself. With his entire self.

## 23.

The bus left at seven in the morning. A total of twenty-three people for the one-day trip to the castles of Ludwig, the mad King. They sat behind a Japanese couple. Throughout the entire journey, she told him about the history of the area and held his hand. Though he was familiar with it all, he let her go on talking, actually encouraging her. The story of that man was one of those that he never tired of hearing again and again. First stop: Neuschwanstein. Presently, inside the chateau, looking at the portrait of the Bavarian monarch, he again saw Helmut Berger, he again confronted that penetrating gaze, the lips like a woman's, the wavy hair and the bad teeth. He recalled what Wagner had said about him: 'He is so courteous and splendid, so exquisite and full of intellect, that his life ought to disappear from this world like a flooding river.' Disappear, like water, like liquid, like that liquid that flows and disappears inside him, like all the liquids inside him, that ceaselessly flow like torrents in all directions.

He watched her as she walked ahead of him mingling with the colourful crowd. She might be any tourist, a tourist in her own country. And he? Why is he here? What power brought him to this place? He gazed out of the window at Lake Starnberg. It was there that Ludwig II had been found drowned one hundred and nine years before. He was just forty-one years old. He looked down at his feet. His boots were covered in slush.

## 24.

Oberammergau. They walk through the streets of the village. He stares at the houses with their painted façades. Young people with clean, bright faces pass them by carrying their ski equipment. A light, irritating rain follows them. Laughing, they make a date for the year 2000 when the village will re-enact Christ's Passion. In the coach, the guide flirts with her: 'Are you attached or is the young man a relative?' His German is poor, but good enough to understand the question. He turns and pretends to give her a stern look. She smiles at him sweetly, takes his arm and puts it round her shoulders. 'You're in no danger, silly,' she says to him. In each other's arms, they gaze out of the window at the snow-covered villages that pass before them.

'Why is it when we're in a car or a train, we say "the landscape's going by"? Why do we say "the landscape's passing before us"?' he asks her. 'In reality, it's we who are passing before the landscape,' he adds on his own.

She looks at him with her grey-green jewels dilated. He bends and kisses her closing his eyes.

Linderhof. Another castle. In a valley lush with vegetation. Wagner in his ears. Inside, the decoration faithfully portrays all the madness of the Bavarian grandeur. The guide fills them with dates and events. He follows behind at the back of the group. He likes watching her as she walks ahead of him. He likes to think of her as something foreign, something that belongs to the group, but something that's his. He, who's simply accompanying her, who's simply present, observing. Hohenschwanstein. The last part of the trip.

During the journey back to the city, she sings, slightly inebriated. A single drop of saliva, hanging as it is from her lower lip, falls and bursts over her grey skirt. He imagines her in ten years' time. Her mouth, unaltered, curls hesitantly into a faint smile, when she in her turn creates a mental picture of him.

# Genesis

## 25.

He's conscious of the world today. And that con-
sciousness is an illness. There are times when
he doesn't pay any attention to it, but now all
around him in the theatre he feels it draining
him, tightening round him, while he has to concentrate on the scene, in this awful perfor-
mance, and she beside him, talking English
with all her friends at the interval on his account and he out of politeness not being able to
give his opinion, 'played-out nonsense, stage de-
piction of Marlene, Marlene wasn't only legs
and liftings, or only cabaret songs, she was the
first to wear men's clothes in films, she was a
friend of Bowie, a complicated female with
every part of her body on the alert', but how

were they to understand, he couldn't put up with them any longer, he felt so stifled that he took her aside and told her he couldn't bear any more, he was leaving, she should stay and they'd see each other at home, and in the depths of his eyes she saw his sorrow saying that shortly his soul would be somewhere that he didn't determine exactly and that now, at precisely that moment, he was at his limit, in five minutes he would have begun to crack, to break up, it's not the play, it's not the people and the work, it's him and the depths of his eyes and other works, truly important ones, and she understood. In order to protect him, she put him into a taxi. As she returned, she felt herself being seized by panic, a spermatic panic in her belly warning her that this humming from his words, together with the love and dizziness, is the same feeling as the one she'd felt earlier in bed. The third bell sounded. The curtain went up. Marlene was reclining with a long cigarette and plunging neckline.

The panic gradually abated. Marlene sighed. The humming was there together with the dizziness. The music began. Marlene got up from the bed. In her bed the feelings were more complicated. And more real.

# 26.

'. . . I'm in Lagonissi in the summer of '64. Oppressive heat and boredom. I wander round the bungalows while the grown-ups are taking their afternoon siesta. I run here and there, I can't keep still. I suddenly see a bird on the roof of one of the bungalows. It's a very strange creature, I've never seen a bird like that, our teacher had never told us anything about birds that were green, grey, red and blue with a bulging breast. I want to touch it, to hold it in my hands. I drag a crate up to the window and with not a little effort I manage to reach the window ledge. Stretching a bit more – I'm pretty agile – I grab hold of the guttering and climb onto what is in any case a low roof. The bird is alarmed and with a weird squawking sound flies off flapping its wings nervily. At that same moment, my foot slips on the wet plaster and I end up hanging in mid-air at a height of two and a half metres, holding on to the gutter. I instinctively look around and to my surprise and alarm I see two tools: a spade lying horizontal on the ground and a pickaxe with one end stuck in the ground and the other sticking upwards, threatening and pointed. Then it was as if time expanded, extended, every second seemed to last an age. Sensing that I was beginning to slip and was heading for an unavoidable fall, the two possibilities flashed through my mind like a film with two endings. The one, landing on the pickaxe, would mean the end. The other would simply mean getting injured. That was the harsh reality. I mustn't panic, I must face it and let myself fall as if it were a bet, like we bet with friends on who'll do the best dive. During the fall, that seemed endless, I felt unexpectedly elated. I surrendered myself to fate, to probability, knowing deep inside me though that I'd survive, that something would happen and I wouldn't fall on the pickaxe. It was as if I were discovering a secret attribute that would accompany me throughout the rest of my life, that would be my secret weapon. That same afternoon, I left the medical centre with a number of superficial injuries to my leg...'


## 27.

The sun's rays enter slantwise, somewhat shyly, from the tiny balcony and gently tickle his face, just enough so that he wakes in an almost relaxed way, in contrast to all the previous days. Despite this, his body aches, his head is heavy, he longs for his house, his room, his country. She's sleeping soundly – she returned late, just before daybreak.

He gets up and makes for the kitchen. He searches for the pots as if blind – he hasn't put his lenses in and everything is filtered through a mist, as if he were looking at a blurred film. The dots disperse and the objects seem dangerously akin: the pan after incessant proddings changes into a strainer, the sugar spoon melts then immediately becomes solid again and changes into a green cup. The shapes and colours move freely, create convenient alliances, get involved in chance associations, dissolve into each other. They exchange thousands of names, names that they gradually reacquire, with patience, just like making a good coffee.

It's a cold day. It's always cold here. The apartment is very small, nicely decorated, though with some hesitancy in the choices. He gazes at the books: psychoanalysis, occult, romantic novellas, palmistry, classics, astrology. A man's photograph. Obviously Tony. Chief executive of ZDF, around fifty, in good shape. On the back of the photo, he reads: 'Ich liebe dich. Tony.' He turns the photo round again and looks more carefully. In another fifteen years, he'll look something like that. All he has to do is watch his diet, exercise and go to bed early. He takes the white bottle from his bag and fills the half-empty cup of coffee. In the mirror, with his lenses now in place, the fairy-tale ends. Never mind fifteen, he won't even have two years left if he carries on like that. He shaves slowly, as if a red dawn were breaking.

## 28.

She had work to do that afternoon. She had to do two private lessons at the other side of town. That allowed him to spend a couple of hours on his own. He had a refreshing hot bath, nibbled something from the fridge, drank two double Absoluts with orange – generous ones since he was in no rush to drink them, there was no danger of anyone seeing him – he got dressed and went out in a much better and calmer mood.

After roaming for quite some time around the bookshops – he bought a novel by Céline in English – around the record shops – he got the latest by the Tintersticks – around two or three beer cellars in Maximillianstrasse and Marienplatz, where he drank lager and ate frankfurters, he turned into a picturesque little street on his way home. He heard voices coming from an old three-storey mansion. The half-erased gothic letters on the sign in the entrance read 'Gallery Genesis: Hindu Welt'. A man dressed in a traditional costume and holding a cane with a gold handle stood in the doorway. He looked like a guard or some such thing. From the little German he knew, he understood that an auction was taking place inside. He entered and found himself in a large room with a wooden floor, red carpet and smells of expensive perfumes. The light was dim; gold particles of dust were held in suspension beneath the heavy chandelier. He looked around him and to his surprise he saw that there were only women in the room. Women of all ages, from adolescents to the extremely elderly, beautiful and ugly, brunettes and blondes, shapely and plump, casual and elegant. He felt their eyes fixed upon him. With great dexterity – the result of long years of practice – he took the small bottle of vodka from his coat pocket and took two large gulps without any of the women noticing.

The elderly woman behind the rostrum announced the next item. The women's attention turned to a strange engraving. It depicted a huge tortoise on which stood six elephants supporting a dish. He felt a shudder pass through him. The tiny tails again began to vibrate erratically. This time he didn't allow himself to be unnerved. He calmly looked around him. The particles of dust had become so dense that they appeared to have formed a cloud. He took out his wallet to check. He'd have to borrow for the remaining two days. Just before the third fall of the hammer, he raised his hand. The women once again turned towards him. As if there were some mutual agreement between them. No one made a higher bid. A quarter of an hour later, he left with the engraving wrapped up. He wouldn't show it to her.

# Haemorrhage

## 29.

*Thanks for making the trip here. I'm sorry I wasn't my real self, that I was so cold and critical; I hope, despite this, that you had a good time, that you saw some new and interesting things. I'm looking forward to seeing you again in Athens. It'll be for longer and we'll be able to come to understand each other better. Thanks for the message you left on the answering machine yesterday. It was so sweet. I was sad at hearing you today on the phone. You sounded so run-down with all the talks, the business, the lawyers and so on. I'd like to be with you to hold you. Please be patient with me, I'm extremely sensitive and exhausted. My nerves are in a mess. I need attention, tenderness and understanding. There's a challenge for you!*

*I miss you.*

Z.

He read it over and over again. I'm sorry ... Thanks ... I was critical ... I need tenderness ... So sweet ... So run-down. Just what had she understood? Could she understand how he'd felt the previous night when he'd been tossing and turning in bed like a madman, with his pulse wavering dangerously, with his thoughts raging like a storm and with the night shattering into pieces, black ones, pitch-black, and falling on the floor and with him trying to save them, but scorching his hands on the burning pieces? And how could he understand the strained nerves, the need for understanding when the light of life comes near to him then immediately goes away again so suddenly, as if wanting to interrupt the darkness only temporarily, to allow him a slight opening for transactions but for so little that it's impossible for him to succeed? How can he, shut up as he is within himself, communicate and sympathize? It's as if he were concealed inside thousands of bodies, thousands of unknown bodies, with which he shares the same life and the same death.

## 30.

New Year's Eve. At last that year is coming to
an end, though with all the windows left open,
letting in the loose ends on all sides, and with
that acute insomnia, the insomnia that's been
lying down beside him for years now, once
again at his side. New Year's Eve, invited to the
party, he in his most convincing wrappings,
smartly dressed, presentable, in an environment
of intellect and power, between the eternal adolescent with the narcissism complex and the language inflexibility, and the neurotic lady with
the sorrowful self-control and unfocused gaze –
two high-profile members of the government –
with him trying to look interested, but hearing
sounds from everywhere, sounds from the open
windows, reminding him of their presence, the
windows with the red frames shouting out, crying urgency, demanding full-speed, together
with the hissing of snakes and the droning of
insects, between the poker and the whisky, with
him winning unstoppably and then quitting,
throwing away the round, betting on a pair.
Completely oblivious to those around him, he
plays only for himself, as if he had no oppo-
nents, he plays as he feels, with colours – when
the colour's green, he stakes his last penny,
when ochre he passes, when blue, he folds. It
seems that the environment, at least in terms of

colour, has affected him as before long he's lost everything. He begins borrowing. At five in the morning, no one will lend him any more. In spite of this, he recalls that the evening has ended somewhat better than the one last year. Then, the new year had found him washed out in bed, watching the digital numbers changing shape.

## 31.

'... We're in Mykonos, the whole family, towards the end of the sixties. It's evening, my folks have gone out on the town. I went to bed at around ten. I'm reading *Little Men* by Louisa May Alcott. I very much liked Dan, the tough guy who drinks and smokes and gambles. The one that's really my sort though is Nat, the orphaned boy who plays the violin to earn pocket-money. I shut the book. I can't get to sleep no matter what. Suddenly, I hear voices in the night. Indistinct at first, then louder. As if someone were suffering, were in pain. I prick up my ears. It must be two people shouting in a strange way, sometimes whispering, sometimes gasping. It reminds me of Nat's restrained crying when, to punish him, his teacher imposes on him an unusual form of punishment: the pupil to hit the teacher ten times with the ruler. At first, Nat hardly touched him, but the teacher insisted, till his hand reddened from the blows of the ruler administered by the pupil. Now, in the night, alone, I'm afraid, but I'm also full of curiosity. I get up and, walking on tiptoe, I make for the door. We're staying in a large house with individual rooms, let by a family. I go out into the corridor. The voices are coming from the room next door. Now they've abated somewhat. They're more like chuckling, expressions more of joy than displeasure. With the innocence and impudence that characterizes me, I turn the knob and witness a scene that freezes my blood: two people, a man and a woman, are lying naked on the bed. She has a very small breast and disproportionately large bottom and is holding the man's willie, which is huge, black and curved upwards. For a moment, the three of us stare at each other rooted to the spot, I, unable to utter a word and they just as they are, dumbstruck. As soon as I recover, I close the door and run back to my room, lock the door and dive beneath the blankets. That night I didn't sleep at all, thinking only of a huge willie held by a thin, delicate hand...'

## 32.

He tries to tidy up the house. He finds it impossible. He feels that his living space is a jigsaw, a jigsaw that can be pieced together in a thousand different ways, of which only one is correct, but that each time he gets close to this, some piece always gets into the wrong place and the whole thing collapses. Sometimes it's the glasses in the bathroom, sometimes the books in the dining-room, sometimes the nail-cutter in the living-room, once he'd even found keys in the fridge. He wonders how things were before, how the presence of the other person affects the place of objects, and he reflects that it is precisely this that has changed, the place – the absence – of the other person from his life. After all, the place of every object reflects the accumulation of memory. The more the memories, the more the messages of absence that collect in his living space, the more the whole overflows, with memories and objects dripping everywhere and, panting for breath, he runs about with plastic buckets to collect all the liquid he can before it manages to submerge the house.

Friends visit him less and less frequently. He receives them seated on the sofa, with the lights dimmed, trying – with great effort it must be said – to maintain a controlled and dignified manner. When the friend goes, he leaves the hollow where he's been sitting on the sofa, without straightening the cover; he leaves it asymmetrically curved to remind him that sitting there just a short while ago, having of his own will chosen to visit him, was a human being who had eaten, drunk and chatted with him. It was that hollow, that crater of memory on the sofa, that still kept him in contact with others.

## Second photograph

'I don't feel well, Bessie...'

'What's up, sis?'

'I don't know, I think it's my fault, my nerves, my health's in a mess, I feel as if I've got 'flu all the time. And not only that ... I feel as if I keep touching something that continually evades me.'

'Him again ... Put an end to it, sis. You can see it's not working out.'

'I can't, I don't want to, I can't...'

'But, really, why do you let it go on? The man's in another world.'

'Listen, Bessie, there isn't always an explanation for everything. Didn't you spend six months with that Lothar in the mountains?'

'What's that got to do with it? Lothar was sick.

Though, from what I've understood, yours is not much better.'

'Are you trying to say that I've made myself responsible for him? Listen, I've become familiar with his needs. Once, as you'll recall, I was there myself – of course I didn't have any help, but I know exactly what it's like when a person can't control himself. It's there that a relationship shows: in the way it holds up when things go wrong.'

'Provided it doesn't boomerang on you. Anyhow, what are you going to do, are you going to Greece?'

'I'll go for a month at least. To see what we're like on a day-to-day basis. There are a few things I don't understand. I feel there's a strange veil over this relationship, a threat all around, like a shadow hanging over us. In bed though it disappears. When we get up again, the vibes change, they're no longer love vibes, they're ... they're something else. But still intense. Look at this! He sent it to me today.'

'This is the next phase. In this one, he must be around twenty-two. In his full prime I see.'

'Look at his gaze. It's askance though he seems to be looking straight ahead. Alone, in the middle of a huge valley.'

He gives me the impression that's he's surrounded. As if he's in a wagon with Indians all around dancing a war dance.'

'If it's like that, then he's organized a good defence. Eyes, nose, mouth lined up to perfection. The entire mechanism of his face on the alert...'

'At first sight, yes. There's something missing though. I'm speaking as a photographer, sis.'

'Yes, you're right, something's missing. Must be the signal for the attack.'

'He looks like a person who keeps everything inside, doesn't he?'

'Yes, he keeps it all inside. It's as if in a strange way he were gestating it. There are people who are pregnant in their soul. And he's one of those.'

# Ikon

## 33.

. . . Over the telephone I had the same feeling that I had while you were here. I turned in on myself on account of your egoism. I feel that the only thing that concerns you is yourself. You talk only of yourself. I feel that if I don't make an effort to articulate a few words of my own, the conversation will be completely one-sided. I have to push you to make you find a little room for me. I imagine that if we live together, it'll be exactly the same. That's how it was when you were here: you didn't listen to the others, whenever anyone said something that wasn't of immediate concern to you, you appeared bored. I read the letter you wrote to yourself in 1988. About your relationship with yourself, about your behaviour to women. Vanity is a very mediocre feeling.

*Repulsive. Have you progressed at all since then? I don't think so. You're still concerned with the same things: personal progress, love, the need for expression. How have they progressed? I don't see you having taken even one step forward.*

*I know this is an unpleasant letter, but I feel angry, and you're the one causing it. Stop focusing on yourself all the time, pay attention to others, to what they say, to their interests, to their needs. You block all this out. It's very, very unhealthy.*

Z.

He read it three or four times. In her previous letter, she'd not been so explicit. She hadn't distanced herself sufficiently. Everything she said he understood completely – in fact he could himself add much more. She'd simply scratched the surface. Not being able to see himself up close – he felt he'd get burned – he tried to focus on his image from a distance.

He saw himself behind a cloud of words. Words that were useless, suspended. A mass of papers with profuse notes flying here and there. He thought that at least he could collect them together in a folder and then later copy them out clearly, file them, put them in a proper order. He owed this tidying up to himself, he owed it to his time. His time, that abstract eventuality, that continual oscillation in the world of probabilities. He took a piece of paper and drew a grid, a right-angled base. When he'd fashioned the boxes, he sat back and looked at them. Not even one word could fit inside.

## 34.

Five in the morning. He'd been awake since four. He knows that any time now she'll be arriving from Europe on the morning flight. She'll be staying for a month. Such a length of time seems to him monstrous, unclassifiable. But he knows there's a door. A gate. And that it's narrow. Of the numerous voices that inhabit this house, he chooses the one that says: 'Be careful!' He paces back and forth in the lounge. His gaze falls on the paintings, on the objects, on the space above the couch. Yes, something's missing there. Above the couch on the white wall he clearly discerns the outline of a painting, the mark of a picture frame that he can't see, all he can see is its place, the space where he has to hang it. 'Where's the content?' he wonders. 'Find it,' he senses a voice instilling the words of command in the hypothalamus.

Yesterday, supposedly by chance, he discovered a wooden horse in the rubbish outside his house. Brown, forty centimetres high, proud, with its leg raised. The veins in its neck bulging, splendour in its eyes, in its movement. He took it home and set it up high to survey the surroundings. Now he stares at it with the blurred eyes of morning, with only two glasses of vodka in his guts, and admits that he was the one to have thrown it out – in fact, he wanted to break it, but felt sorry for it, or rather he censored the act's sentimentality. He'd begun playing games with his own self, games that were peculiar but necessary. The downstairs doorbell rang shrilly in the morning calm. He looked through the video camera. She was standing there nervily, looking travelled, with obvious impatience and two large suitcases. He looked at her again. He felt like in the films. Except that in this case the heroine would step down from the screen into his arms. He reached out and pressed the button.

# 35.

'... Summer in Andros, at the end of the sixties, I've just come back from the sea and I'm alone in a huge garden full of violets, pansies, daisies and various kinds of wonderful flowers. It's unbearably hot, I want to get the salt off me. I get the hose pipe, turn on the tap, take off my trunks and begin to wash myself down. As the fresh water falls over me and surrounded as I am by those dreamy fragrances from the flowering garden, alone and naked, I feel a sort of added warmth, despite the cool water running down my body. It's a new sensation, warmth and chill at the same time. I feel as if I belong to something bigger, to something that embraces me and the garden and the house, together with the story by Dickens that I was reading – Pip and Estella and Miss Havisham – as if they were all contained in this huge one that dwelt in my naked body. I can still feel that entire sensation focusing there down below, as if it were the tube connecting me with the rest of the world bringing me the smells, the warmth, the stories and the chill. Suddenly my friend Spyros opens the iron garden gate. Spyros and I usually showered together, yet for the first time I feel that his presence is disturbing all that peace and beauty, and with a quick, embarrassed movement, I put my trunks back on out of shame. Afterwards, I felt very bad and I couldn't understand why we stop feeling that way when someone else is present. I decided, however, to repeat it with the girl who took care of us and I immediately saw the difference...'

# 36.

Their life was ostensibly like that of any couple. For a while they did what the English call 'play house'. They shopped together, cooked, she went to the local gym, he played basketball in the neighbourhood, albeit as a chore, they went to the cinema, theatre, concerts, they occasionally had people round to the house, and then, presenting a reasonably dignified outward image, they appeared as a not uninteresting couple, with views, humour, personality. In their private moments, though, the pattern was reversed. Continual tension, quarrels, tears, with the only source of relief being the bed, where in a magical way everything was settled.

One Saturday they went to a concert of classical music – it was a friend of the family who was playing – and there they ran into a couple they knew. Fotis was a journalist, three years older, thin, with an angular intelligent face. With him was Dessie, a nondescript girl who designed jewellery. They went somewhere in Kaisariani to eat. There they got into a terrible argument – he was the one who started it – for no good reason, some criticism Dessie had made about the concert, as if he were an expert on classical music – an argument that erupted when it got onto Fotis and their relationship. In a merciless full-frontal attack, he accused him of indifference, of taking advantage, of undermining, of ... of ... whatever likely and unlikely issue she could get into the bag of complaints and failings, of problems that – supposedly piling up for years – were now pouring out inflated and poisonous. In fact, nothing of what he said was of any real interest to him. He didn't care about Fotis and their relationship, or the concert or Dessie, nor about her either. He was vying with his own self. One by one, he descended the steps to the basement where he'd hidden his last bottles. When he'd finished, he felt as if he'd swallowed shark bait, foul-smelling bait, full of poison, that turned his guts. He went home and slept in the bathroom wrapped up in a blanket, with his head resting on the toilet basin. He had no dreams.

# Jackals

## 37.

He's alone with his enemies. Deep within their circle, completely alone, unprotected. On the floor fear has etched a ground plan with a knife. That's his home, his fortress. That's where he moves. The outer walls are burning, tiny flames shoot out from between the joints of the bricks. The ceiling, an oscillating blade, descends threateningly towards his neck. The floor is a raft on which he's floating. With chairs and kitchenware he fends off the monsters patrolling behind the skirting-board. The light fittings, huge searchlights, incessantly roam the landscape. The bookcases block the window stopping any ray of sun from wheedling its way in. The door leading to a semi-private balcony is an electrified area. The front door, the sole escape, is well-guarded. Outside the house is a group of semi-naked men with sharp swords and colourful flags. They are mounted on camels, griffins, unicorns, tigers, jackals, boars and are racing round and round shouting inarticulately. Birds of all kinds are intermingled with the bodies and the animals. Dust, tramping, a smell of burning fill the area. It is a festival of death. And he is the prize.

Late, at around eleven, she wanted something to eat. He made her an omelette. The tiny tails started to vibrate again and reminded him of the island. When she was leaving. He'd kept the receipt from the café. Together with the plan she'd given him showing him where to find her at the airport. He cooked the omelette in a frenzy, as if commenting through his movements on the whole process. By the end, the kitchen was a shambles: onions on the floor, eggs dripping in the fridge, peppers in the sink, knives and forks thrown here and there. The omelette was superb though, she later reflected. The cost, of course, was that she had to clear up the kitchen. That's how it was with him. Any good deed, any little pleasure had to be paid for twice over. And yet she was still here, pushed by that strange need to see things through to the end, to untangle the thread, to complete the mission, the one that she'd tried in vain to explain to her sister. A great mission, to which she was pledged. With mathematical precision, with a surgeon's skilful movements, she was leading him to the end. She was helping him to explode, to diffuse, to understand.

# 38.

You'll either change or come to an end, he thought. You've no other solution. Better the end than this coma. Accepting all the humiliation and degradation from your uncoordinated self, cramming all the shame of a past age, another long-gone age, almost lost, into this one. How can you wear time's clothing inside out? How far from the weight of the real world is the weight of your own? Wheezing, the mind, once the ruler, supporting the mirror of the once lofty spirits with the gilt frame, crawling on all fours, and the last thoughts being born low down, so low, on a level with the ground. There's a motionless position there in the depths of your sleep that calls you. It waits for you to bury yourself inside. From there, to see calmly at some point, at a distance, your unregulated body in flames, together with the jasmine and the foreign girl.

'How are you?'

'Fine.'

'I've given you all I have to give. I've nothing more.'

'Me, I don't know, I don't know how to give.'

'I believed you. I still do.'

'I've no doubt. I'm sure of it. You can't understand me. No one can. You can't connect ... When all those thoughts have to take shape ... I don't belong here. You and your kind ... you fashion a mask and you adapt it. I'm not like that. I can't. I don't belong here. I've nothing in common...'

'So this is where you've come to? So low, I wouldn't have imagined it. You should have told me from the beginning. I wouldn't have imagined it...'

# 39.

He can't stay inside any longer. He's suffocating, he wants to go out, but not with her. But nor with others either. He'll go to the cinema, alone as always in the dark auditorium, lost in another dream, with his immune system at the lowest level, his immune system completely disrupted by the fierce attack of the alcohol, powerless before the images that enter through the eyes and ears and that assail him, contaminate him, as they pass straight into his veins and rapidly spread throughout the organism. Intravenous images that move in slow, digressive scenes within a galaxy of warm colours, predominantly orange, and are spinning. Time, history and Kusturica's film become one with his condition, one with his isolation and with his feelings that he fixes to the root, the root of the tree that is his sorrow.

He goes home on foot in the rain. He doesn't remember anything special from the film. Before opening the door, he goes over to the radiator cupboard in the corridor. It's the only place he has left to hide his bottles. She's found all the other hiding-places, even the one under the boxes of old books on the back balcony. The cupboard is empty. She's become an expert, her mind works in co-ordination with his lies. He opens the door and sees her lying in a strange position in the couch with an awkward smile. What he'd imagined had happened. And of course during the one time that he was out. He'd had the expected telephone call from the past. And she'd answered it. The strange thing is that he feels such relief as if he'd caused it. He no longer cares about anything. The iceman settles in his body. The images begin to spread. The contamination advances all over.

# 40.

He was now almost certain that she loved him;
that she loved him deeply, more than she'd ever
loved anyone in her life. No one puts up with so
much and in such a short time, without any
reciprocation, any expectation. He was terrified
by that love; he felt as if it were laying claim to
the only relationship he'd managed to hold on
to: his relationship with his inner eye, that
sleepless gaze that day and night followed his
movements, that perfectly round eye that he'd
once swallowed and that since then had been
continually watching him.

He felt that it was as if she were saying to
him that I'm the one who was born to show you
what your life is like, I'm the one who's going
to save you, because I know, because I've been
where you're at, because I have the answers,
because I'm the only one able to see that in this
soul there's panic and expectation and destruc-
tion and freedom; that this life can't be verified
like that, that it doesn't deserve such an end.

'I had a dream,' she said to him one morning
after coffee. 'I'd come from abroad and you
came by car to collect me from the airport.
Instead of taking me to the centre, you headed
off towards Mount Parnitha, you had something

important you wanted to tell me. We left the car a couple of kilometres before Mont Parnasse Casino, at an old abandoned inn, and we walked along the side of a small river. You were talking excitedly about me, you had schemes, you had ideas for new things, you'd made plans ... You talked to me non-stop. I listened and watched the dirty water and discarded cans, without believing you. I was playing with a twig that I'd broken off and was throwing bits of it one by one into the water. When they'd all gone, you asked me: 'Why did you come?' And then I turned and looked at you. You were walking one step behind me and I saw the knife in your hands – I knew that knife well because it was my mother's, a large kitchen knife that we used to hide from her in case she had a fit. You looked calmly into my eyes, first time I'd seen you so calm, yet I wasn't afraid, not that I knew, but I tried to make myself aware of what I was feeling and I sensed the earth falling wet and the noise of the wood getting louder and I opened my arms in embrace and I took you entire inside me, the whole of you and the knife too.'

# Kaleidoscope

## 41.

'... I've gone on my own to the cinema. I'm eleven years old. I'm watching the musical version of Dickens' *Oliver Twist*. Mark Lester is playing Oliver. Dickens is my favourite author at that time. *David Copperfield, Nicholas Nickleby, Great Expectations*. I also like Walter Scott, and *Crime and Punishment*. In general, I read a great deal, all day with a book in my hands. At school I'm bored, because everything the teachers say I already know, I've read it long before. I can't believe how stupid the other kids are. What do they do all that time? I see that I can play football, quarrel, go swimming in the summer and read. What do they do? They must be completely stupid; which is why when I'm bored during the lesson, I annoy them and sometimes set about them. But I'm the best pupil and so for the time being they forgive me.

Sitting next to me in the cinema is a girl. She's on her own too. Last year it wouldn't have surprised me, but this year I feel strange. I look at her out of the corner of my eye – peripheral vision was always my speciality, my eyes have always worked like complex optical instruments. She's on the thin side, with a slender nose and large dark eyes. She's wearing a check shirt and a light blue skirt. She seems totally absorbed in the film, as I am too, though gradually and ingeniously we've moved closer to each other. The ground for our flirting is the arm between the seats that we both lay claim to with remarkable determination. So that eventually our elbows unavoidably come into contact and we feel each other's warmth. Towards the end of the film, we've both turned our bodies towards the other and, in the scene where Oliver wakes up in the house of the wealthy man and for the first time finds himself in a warm environment far from the thieves and the coffins where he'd been sleeping, our heads softly touch and we watch the last twenty minutes like that. When the lights go up, the girl jumps up and disappears in the wink of an eye, without even casting a glance at me. I find it unbelievable...'

## 42.

She senses him pulling away, becoming distant.
She feels that he still hasn't calmed down, he
hasn't overcome things that are no longer of his
age, things he should have come to terms with
long before. Though he's suffering deep inside,
he doesn't seem to want her sympathy. It's as if
he were looking for pain everywhere, trying his
best to suffer. Each new day inters the previous
one in fresh earth. She gazes at him as he lies
beside her on the bed one Sunday afternoon.
He's watching football – his team, the reds, who
do nothing but lose. As she watches him, appar-
ently normal, calm, concentrating on the game,
she wonders at how this can be the same person
who only yesterday was shaking and weeping,
who swore at her, belittled her and who afterwards in bed was as sweet and tender as any
man she'd ever met in her life. How was it that
that wave that swept the bed abated as soon as
they got up, that that rapidly spreading, frantic
flow settled, subsided, got bogged down. Just
what kind of mourning is it that comes and goes
without any regularity? Looking at him, she has
the impression that a fine thread is stretched
across him linking him with the earth. This is
the thread he leaves free to be tugged by every
passing breeze. He's like a child who can't concentrate, has no aim. He true self has become a

plaything, a toy in the hands of this habit, this force controlling him, the same one that punishes him and will go on punishing his mind and soul till it has finished, however and wherever and if ever this unequal campaign finishes. Till the final battle, with the javelins and flamethrowers, on the battlefields of Gaugamela or Grammos, with mantles or greatcoats, in whatever place his imagination has prepared the ground for the final confrontation.

Suddenly, something startles her. She feels him moving close to her. As if he were reading her thoughts and telling her that she doesn't have the right, she doesn't have the knowledge, she's not aware of the cause, the persons, the history. She looks him in the eye. And she shudders. She shudders because this is the same person who in a rare moment in front of the television, when calm and rested, will hug her tenderly and kiss her ear with a whisper that says everything.

## 43.

During the return journey from the airport everything is still open. The sadness the same, uprooted now, almost visible, love outflanked, with elevation's wings crushed, the illness spreading. Thirty days and nights a daily routine and then alone again, once more back at the beginning. He tries to say something to the taxi driver. Nothing comes out, as if the words flow from his mouth in reverse, roll down the tongue, are led by the oesophagus directly into the stomach, are swallowed unprocessed with a feverish greed, in an uncontrolled ritual which will be consummated later at home, when with unstoppable violence his organism will vomit them up and will remain paralysed. It is these images of violence, these kaleidoscopic images of horror that he feels within, which accumulate in his stomach in short sentences, in paragraphs, in monosyllabic morphemes. It's his speech that wants to stuff him as deep as it can, to cram his mouth with these indescribable expressions, to pump up his body's storeroom to such a degree as to precipitate the day that he'll throw up the last, liberating, Great Vomit and then he'll see himself in the mirror, see his image, he'll see that imprint that wriggles and whines – a poor creature pretending to be something tragically real, that imitates whatever fortune presents it with, in a way that scourges its heart, that ruins it, that violently severs it from a love, like an unripe fruit, and changes it. In this time of wilderness in which he lives, in shades of light blue moments that flicker, he breathes in the smell of the city's blue, at the centre of an epidemic that only he sees and that he shares with the rosy animals that visit him in his sleep.

# 44.

*'All children, except one, grow up.'*
— J. M. Barrie, *Peter Pan*

He sat all day in the dark living-room, with just one orange light lighting the wall. Through the balcony door he could see the house opposite, the housewife watering the flowers, the daughter getting the evening meal ready. He'd spent the whole of the previous day at the hospital, at the side of his father, who'd just come out of an operation. With him was the whole family and his younger cousin, Theoni, who'd lost her voice six months ago as a result of a great disappointment – she was the sweetest of things, a sculptress, and he was extremely fond of her. That evening he took her out to eat and told her the story of Peter Pan. He felt as if he were out with a child, even though Theoni was twenty-three. He spoon-fed her the dessert and she stared at him with large eyes, eyes that have looked happiness in the face, and he shuddered at the thought that he, though much older than her, had never confronted that gaze in which the pupil embraces the iris and spreads the vitreous humour in the socket in concentric circles.

That evening he turned off the light and went out. He went to a bar at the back of Stadiou Street. While climbing up the inner staircase, he felt the temperature rising at an exponential rate. He was perspiring and his hands still had that slight trembling that he sought to calm with a double vodka. To the right of the bar was a heavy wooden door. He noticed that every so often various people opened it and went inside. After the third drink, he tried it himself. He found himself in a pitch black room. Immediately, he sensed that he wasn't alone. There were a number of people inside there in the darkness. He could hear soft voices, sighing. He realized what it was and proceeded till he felt a wall and leaned against it. A strong acidic smell mixed with an indefinable aroma spread throughout the room. Before long he felt a hand stroking his head. He clutched at it immediately and, after making sure it was a female one, he searched for the mouth. It was there, in its place, just like all the rest.

# Lethargy

## 45.

*Dearest,*

*It's a marvellous sunny day, the snow and cold winds have gone. I've been here in London a week now. I came from one world to another, which increases the variety of impressions and pleases me. I miss you just as I miss our tender, intimate moments. I hope you'll come to London and we'll experience them again. Yesterday, I went to see 'Sense and Sensibility'; I liked it a lot. Subjects such as marriage, love, comfort, prejudice, judgement, feelings and their discovery, and how to find a balance between passion and reason are of prime importance for me. When you come, we'll go to the cinema and hold hands. Like in Athens. So lovely ... Lately, I've been thinking a lot about that platitude, that love doesn't only have to do with giving and supporting, but also with accepting the personality of the other, with accepting his needs. With you, I was suddenly faced with characteristics that shocked me, like the drink, the self-centredness, the refusal of any form of compromise, the personal chaos, the sense of superiority. There's no doubt that these are matters that I'd eventually have to come to terms with. I've thought a lot about the month we spent together. About what happened, about the roles we both played. It was all very intense. I felt you were attacking my life, my friends, matters of my health, my intellectual beliefs. It was like being in a battlefield twenty-four hours a day.*

*I look forward to seeing you soon.*

Z.

*P.S. Love you but won't leave you, as the saying goes.*

'Dearest'. She's still calling him that. He thinks of her sitting in her wooden chair, on her earthly throne, before the mirror, with the eyeliner and powder, looking at herself and observing her face, her nose, that she doesn't like, her eyes, with the tiny wrinkles surrounding them; looking at herself and in her face seeing his need, her need, her need for him, his need for her. She often catches herself consciously removing him from his pedestal, including him as just one more piece in the mosaic of her experiences, one more piece of material to be processed; imagining him as a piece of time. Though of empty time. Those who think they've been through everything don't understand the meaning of empty time. Time again. And its emptiness. The deepest, continuous emptiness. Black, white and nothing. Emptiness is not nothing. Emptiness has components, it's made up of parts. Just as experience is a collection of minor events, so too emptiness is a collection of tiny refusals, of tiny buts and nos, which come and weave themselves as threads of negation to fashion the 'not now', the elsewhere. And she, for him, is now elsewhere, the mirror whispers to her, not without a little irony.

# 46.

Heathrow. Patches of ice in the morning, almost daybreak, corridors, escalators, claustrophobic atmosphere, police with machine-guns, colourful tourists, thick smoke spreading from the capital, a smell of naphthalene from the city's innards, his pupils wet, contracted. The end of February, here again after seven years. A dry breath flays the throat, he feels that welcome morning liquid that circulates again in the blood after ten hours' abstinence.

He catches the bus to Victoria. It's a journey he's made at least twenty times. The hotels close to the airport, the small football pitches, the council estates. He recalls the Eighties. 'We will use London as a laboratory,' said Hugo from the University. In the end it was he who'd used London as a field for experimentation – experimentation in cohabitation, in abandonment, in acquaintances, particularly the one before last, who'd brought him to where she'd brought him and was now recycling him, and here he was again, with the dry snow covering the rooftops and the bitter exhalations (or exhortations) coming out of the poisoned orifices. He gasps, winces at the English light, accustoms himself again to the chloride-filled fog that ranges slowly, almost sarcastically. A violet glow illumines everything, a flame with a skin-smooth outline consumes the landscape, the muddy green streams and the ruddy-faced people. The bus halts at the first traffic light of the city. A dark-skinned boy in tattered clothes crosses the road. He is wearing a green sweater with some group's name and a torn leather jacket. In his hand he's carrying a top hat. David Copperfield winks at him. He walks with the furtive step of a feline. From afar, he can discern a hungry yellow spite in his eyes. He knows that look. It's his; he still has it benumbed inside him.

## 47.

A walk through the town. Together with her. They pass by the little wood, cross the garden of the red brick school – the wire netting is still there, with the hole in the same spot; still there too is the place where he used to play football with George. Further on is his old street and the house where he lived ten years before. Everything just the same and completely unchanged, at least outwardly. Mr Clein's car with the sign for use by disabled people, the garden, always untidy, the second floor with the marks of the fire. In the same neighbourhood, the 7–11 owned by the Greek, the wine bar with snails, the pub. In the wider area, the Everyman cinema, the Dome, Dingwalls. He can clearly see the mark of the cut. The vertical incision that opened up his chest to the man. England, his first contact with a life of luxury and a lack of motivation, the letting-go, the fraught glances all around, the plunge into the white liquid. And afterwards the light that shone dimly, the wrong choice, the waiting, the irritation, the acceptance, the giving, the stagnancy, the boredom, the rift. And now the strain, the limit, the *déjà vu*. England's a strange place. Just as the manner of its people, so too the light is full of innuendo. Perhaps it's precisely this light that also shapes their allusive manner. Under this umbrella of sidelong glances, he took his first steps in a new world. It didn't matter that it lasted for only a short time, that it failed. What matters is that now he's here again, in the same place with a third woman, giving rise, as always happened, to one more coincidence in his life. Striving to again create the same conditions so that the Other would be baptized in the same water, receive communion from the same hand. Only one thing escaped him: that this here was her place. She was here long before him and she knew her way around much better.

# 48.

On the third day they went to a party in Chelsea. It was given by the son of a Professor at Oxford University, a friend of hers from her student days. He dressed appropriately, took an enjoyable hot bath in the tub, shaved and, in his newly-bought clothes from Camden Town, looked very respectable, even charming. His face, though somewhat swollen from the alcohol, had regained something of its shine; his eyes flirted with their old scintillating expression; his mouth, less taut, could relax into a pleasant smile. He did a few exercises, but his body was still bowed, in a position of supplication, in a gradual attempt to bend, till it reached the ground, which as it seems was its final destination.

At the party, she quickly disappeared among dozens of friends. He, by nature observant, found himself a corner and with drink in hand stared at the crowd of intellectuals with their characteristic pose, their self-complacency mixed with insecurity, their affectation in movement and speech. He felt as if he were part of the stage set for a BBC serial or a James Ivory film. He went up to a tall, blonde girl, on the plump side, with intelligent green eyes, who appeared to be alone.

'Do you work at the university?' he asked.

'No, I'm an artist.'

'Have you had any exhibitions?'

'Just one at the Kensington Gallery.'

'What do you paint?'

'I don't paint exactly. I do installations.'

'Well then, the environment here must inspire you. It's an installation in itself.'

'You're not far wrong,' she said laughing. 'Are you her boyfriend...?'

'Yes, I think so.'

'You seem very young. I imagined you older.'

'I am older.'

'I've known her since primary school. She's a very sensitive girl. I hope you won't hurt her.'

'Do I seem the type to hurt women?'

'You seem the type to walk around with a penknife.'

'Oh, you noticed it, I see!'

'It's sticking out of your back pocket,' she said laughing and disappeared into the installation.

# Melancholy

## 49.

Visit to her sister's house in Kensington. Z. and
Bessie. Two sisters who, apart from the fact that
they have the same mother and father, have
nothing else in common. The one a dreamer,
self-assured, clever, energetic, but saddened,
tired and in a corner. The other, a girl *comme il
faut*, conservative, well-mannered, with a chame-
leonic social behaviour, superficial – yet para-
doxically a very good photographer. How would
she be in bed, he wondered. Probably giving,
she'd perform what is usually described as enjoyable sex. What, as long as it lasts, is good,
even very good, and then you want to disappear
as quickly as possible till the next time, when
you hope that all the preliminaries and/or going

out won't be necessary. He knew that type of woman very well, since, because of special circumstances, he always happened to be surrounded by representatives of it. His contact with them was never good, though often, particularly in sexually-lean periods, he resorted to their feigned tenderness, so that the results were catastrophic both for his emotions and his sense of aesthetics – yes, he even had a little of this at times. This is what passed through his mind as he gazed at the brimming glass that invited him to empty it. And it was then that the inevitable happened: with a clumsy movement, he knocked over the glass and the vodka spilled over Bessie's expensive gold and red carpet. Her sister flushed, mumbled something in German – 'Griechische schwein!' – a compliment that he understood immediately, and, furious, sprang to her feet with a threatening look. Terrified, Z. tried to smooth things over. He, rather sadistically, went on with 'Eh, never mind, it's only liquid, it'll dry, what were we saying?' greatly revelling in the whole situation and playing with the wrought nerves of the younger, hysterical sister. The evening ended badly, in the same way that Bessie passed through his life. He remembered her later, when after two months had passed, she wrote to him in Athens with a photocopy of the cleaner's bill, asking – demanding – that he send her the amount to London. Of course, he never did. It was a question of upbringing. But also of aesthetics.

## 50.

He'd known them for the past twenty years. He'd met them here – family friends – they get together now and again, they were witnesses to his first adventure, that ended in the same foggy city ten years ago, and the second, the more recent one, which over the last few days had been gradually vanishing from his mind. Now once again, with her this time, he's visiting them in a weird state, despondent, with his heart in a thousand pieces, distant, speaking using a confused vocabulary and confusing meanings, flinging out incoherent sentences and then again trying to find the thread, a thread though that's lost for good in poorly designed, clumsy verbal labyrinths. On the other hand, how strange it is that, though self-destructive and dried up, full of alarm and despair, with his very foundations being eaten away by the worst form of erosion, he should be able at the same time to observe all this from outside – for this in fact was what was happening all this time: he was watching his fall, to make this hypodermic journey in reverse in his despair, to rationalize, to record the stages of his decomposition and so justify the role he's chosen for himself: that of an excavator, a digger into his own being.

His friends are alarmed. They realize how much worse he is than on the previous occasion. But they don't show it. They're fond of him, accept him, answer him as if nothing was amiss. Recognizing this conventional tolerance, he buries whatever's left of his remorse and, silently thanking them, continues that frivolous show, that agreed capriciousness, with the three others looking askance in collusion and he, with each new wave of uncontrollable verbiage, fatally turning in on himself and feeling his breath caught, his guts dark, his bile black, all the ingredients of melancholy.

51.

From the small balcony in Sloane Square, he gazes at the few passers-by. The London middle-classes who've just finished work and are on their way home for the evening game-shows: 'The Price is Right', 'Blind Date', 'A Question of Sport'. Perhaps they're going to the pub for the first pint of the evening. This will be followed

by countless others, till, at five to eleven, the terrible, compulsive bells will ring lowering a wet
curtain on the enjoyment, 'Last orders' ... He
doesn't need any such sound effects, he has his
own exclusive, mobile and personal off-licence.
Besides, he never did like social drinking. He
always preferred to be alone, just him and the
bottle, face to face, without any distractions.

He remarks that it's a particularly cold day.
He shuts the window and goes back into the
living-room with his glass half-empty.

It was a familiar end that he was striving to
find in London. He wanted to direct things so
that the whole business would once again come
to a head in the same place. To lure the enemy
into the same spot and there where the other
thinks that the last battle, the final reckoning,
will take place, there to surrender, to present
the other with his complete fall, offering in this
way an unexpected alternative solution. And
afterwards, if he has time, if there's still time, to
retreat, regroup and counterattack. In a battle of
this kind, there's no shilly-shallying. Everything
here is authentic, risk is risk and pain pain.

He'd had a lot of dreams since coming to
London, as if they'd travelled over with him
from Greece, dream-guides, the first inklings
that would later grow. It's in this phase that he

leaves the first clear mark on his story, that which will delineate a containing space, a cross-section of the edifice that is his life, a division of the chosen microcosm where his self resides, with the lines of the incision – the bones – blacker than black from the thickest ink and the heart sketched on the back wall with a faint projected outline. It is a geometrical shape with two axes, rather like a warped circle. An ellipse.

## 52.

The last evening in London. In the afternoon, her mother had phoned her. He noted that she spoke to her hurriedly, hardly able to hold back her tears. Then she shut herself in the bathroom for half an hour. He asked her what had happened, she was evasive. Her face didn't show any signs of her being upset. Her bearing upright, her limbs in place, her joints well greased. The mechanism of her existence appeared already to have assimilated the bitterness. As he looked at her, she seemed to him like a living, personified symbol, a symbol of dignity and patience, a proud, positive, despondent person. Lying down with her knee bent, she talked of totally unconnected things, her work, her home, the new decoration, the film they'd seen the previous day. He observed her, lying as she was naked on her back, while he, sitting beside her, caressed her hand. Over the bed was a picture from the frontispiece of a book by the Dutch astronomer Andreas Cellarius, which depicted Copernicus, Ptolemy and Galileo with four cherubs above them holding a parchment on which was written 'Harmonia Macrocosmica'. Everything was so still, so calm that for a moment, it was as if his self emerged from within and as if his eyes rose up and stared at them together as they talked and caressed each other on a bed in a small room in a bourgeois neighbourhood in a northern European capital, both of them knowing that circulating in their touch is a dense, humbled time.

In the end, they didn't go out. They stayed in, watched television, made love, he didn't drink too much and cooked for her, being careful not to make a mess of the kitchen. In the morning, he didn't wake her. He left her a note – 'Our next evening will be in the mountains in front of the fireplace' – and he left for the airport, taking his bottles with him.

# Third photograph

'Rude, inept ... How can you? You don't suit each other. There's something quite unbearable about him, he's arrogant, uncouth. He's also too young for you in my opinion. As for his behaviour...'

'It's not that. He's really very egocentric, he lives in his own world, he recognizes no one. And yet it's only with him that I can talk about those things that really matter to me. It's amazing, Bessie, but he may be in a state of lethargy, he may talk more or less on his own, fight with shadows, feed his own aggressiveness, shout, swear yet suddenly, when something appeals to him, when he feels that something the other one says touches his heart and mind, he undergoes a transformation. He suddenly becomes sober, he listens, moderates his words, even his voice and expression change. And at the first friction, the first difficulty, his face shows him crushed once again and he completely collapses. It's like the torment of Sisyphus. He walks up a hill carrying a load, only for it to roll back down again. Except that not even he knows what he's carrying any more. And how could he know when he, his own self, is that load?'

'What do you intend doing?'

'I'm going one more time to Athens. To see who he really is. One last trial. I've made up my mind. Either we'll reconcile things or I'm leaving for good.'

'Whatever you think best. But in my opinion you've absolutely nothing in common. That man can't give, he doesn't want to offer anything. He hasn't learned how to be with others. Look, it's only too clear in this photo. How old is he here?'

'Around twenty-five. He's in London. That must be his former girlfriend. Look how, although he has his arm round her, his gaze, his mind seem to be elsewhere. He's only quasi present.'

'Yes, he's also much heavier, bloated; he seems to be suffering. They're all looking at the lens, while he's on the left, out of the shot, as if shy, as if he doesn't belong to the surroundings.'

'That's him all right; solitary and social, aggressive and charming, indifferent and amorous. I can't stand the torment of that kind of relationship any longer. I've had enough of all the ups and downs. I want a partner who's stable, calm and creative. I'll go to Athens just one more time. I hope my intuition is proved wrong, but I've a feeling that it'll be the last time.'

'I hope so, for your own good.'

# Nemesis

## 53.

'...A park bench in Mavilis Square. I'm out on a date with a girl I met in Hydra in the summer. She came to Greece just a year before, after the fall of the Junta. Her family took refuge in Paris while the Junta was in power. We've begun a relationship, we hold hands, kiss on the lips, go out in mid-week. Now we're arm in arm on a park bench facing the Mikés pâtisserie and I'm trying to persuade her to come home with me. I'm fondling her neck, gently touching her breast over her jumper. Looking straight ahead, she encourages me to hold her, is slightly embarrassed by my fondling, and pulls my hand from her breast. After an hour's pestering, she finally agrees to come home with me. We sit on the couch, I lower the lights. I put Rod Stewart on the record player. "Tonight's the night." Then I go into the kitchen to make her a coffee. I pour an orange juice for myself. I tip half of it out and fill the rest with vodka. I stir it well so the mixture will seem homogeneous. I take a good gulp and go back into the lounge. Before long we're on the carpet. I caress her between her legs outside her jeans. She puts up little resistance. She kisses me on the lips, her hand goes down to my chest, keeps going as far as my waist, reaches to my buttocks, till finally she touches me on the vital spot. Feeling liberated, I help her with the zip. Halfway through, I see her eyes filling with tears. She pulls her hand away and gets up. She quickly fixes her hair and comes out with a sharp "I have to go". Without saying a word, I escort her to the front door, while the record has stuck at the line of a song: "The first cut is the deepest". Divine Retribution, I wonder...'

# 54.

*...I can't wait to go to your place in the mountains, to go for long walks. Fresh air and a natural life! That's just what I need right now. I hope it*

*works out better this time. I was glad that you said in your letter that you've decided to change, to help yourself. I hope you start paying some attention to the needs of others too. When I tell you over the phone that I don't feel well, you mumble a couple of words and change the subject. Something's not right there. Your problem is accepting, coming to terms with things. If I can't tell my partner that I'm not feeling well, who can I tell? Why do I have to continually hide behind a mask pretending that nothing's the matter? We have to talk about all this. It's very important. I'm hoping this time to see your true self, whatever that is, whatever it means. No more drink, no more feelings of superiority, no more masks. Your real self. I want to see you caring, to see you concerned. I want you to cook for me, take care of me, to take me out somewhere nice to eat one night.*

*I'm thinking of you. See you soon.*

Z.

She likes writing to him very much. He counts her letters – he's kept them all in a folder. That's the thirtieth. Thirty letters in six months. Not counting the cards. He imagines her at her desk leaning over the white paper; first wondering about the tone that she should use, then deciding, then hesitating, then beginning with great care, as if wanting to keep a balance, then remembering some instance of disagreeable behaviour on his part, becoming angry and scribbling away. First calling him 'dearest', 'partner', and then while writing, making a complete about-turn, attacking him, rejecting him. Yet she appears to have decided on it. She'll write to explain to him how she feels with him. She'll write each time as she feels about him, as she wants him, as she resists him. Correspondence for her is another kind of communication. But for him writing is a different matter altogether. It's revenge. The revenge of the fingers.

## 55.

His heart felt as if it would burst. 'Yes,' he said, 'yes, it's what I want. Yes. I want it to end.' He stood before the mirror holding the shaving foam and the silver razor – a gift from her. His white dressing-gown, with two or three tears up the side, dragged over the light-blue tiles. He lifted his eyes and a fuzziness spread through his head. He couldn't keep his balance, he felt he was suffocating. A sharp pain began from his mouth and, flaying his oesophagus, ended in his left side, which, unnaturally swollen, appeared to want to explode. His tongue was all white; red and black marks adorned his eyelids.

A cockroach passed quickly in front of the base of the tap. He took the belt from his dressing-gown and tried to chase it off, hitting at it with the belt. He hit and the belt became soaked, but he continued with an incredible fury, till his legs gave way and he slipped, falling on his back.

He remained there for quite some time, trapped, unable – and not even wanting – to get up, gazing at the white ceiling and feeling that of all his senses, his hearing is the one that he's lost, as he couldn't hear, not one sound, only his heartbeat and that not inwardly through the ear, through the cerebellum, but osseously, through the bones, through their creaking.

The sea, he thought, the sea and the tiny tails, the sea and the flowers and lanes on the island, all in ochre and blue, and the jasmine, and when he kissed her and abandoned all excuses and inhibitions, thinking here I am, this is me now – believing that everything hinged on that moment; and that's how it was and he felt that yes, she's the one, and he saw her, her eyes too said 'yes' and he pulled her to him and once again his heart felt as if it would burst.

# 56.

*'La chair est triste, hélas! et j'ai lu tous les livres.'*
– Stéphane Mallarmé, 'Brise Marine'

And now the final act. Whatever happens, he'll shut it hermetically inside him for ever; nothing will remain between him and the bottom of the sea – or the mountain's crater. Nothing. At present, before the final move, his daemon is calm. It stands at a distance and watches. Every so often, it makes some comment – in a superior tone, it's true – as if telling him that it's quite plain now, that the only solution is a catharsis, an underwater catharsis, a final dive to the bottom of his liquid nature. He, of course, swears that he won't hurt her any more; he's sorry for her, feels for her, recognizes her sensitivity, her intellect, her constant emotional tilling, nevertheless he relies precisely on this mystical, introvert feature. What leads her to interpret this peculiar behaviour, the drowning in the daemonic liquid and the hope of rebaptism as a cathartic ritual, a launching ritual at which she herself will preside, will officiate. Their chemistry, their 'karma', as she puts it, is the one thing that can bring him face to face with reality. She's extremely apprehensive about these four days. He's promised her a trip to his blossoming mountain village, calm and concentration. It's the liquid dream, however, that has the upper hand. The place where they're going won't be a sanatorium. It'll be an arena.

The day that they had agreed arrived. Ostensibly, it appeared calm. They spend a first night of truce at home and the next day they would leave for the mountain. They slept in separate beds – she wanted it, on some pretence – each of them clutching at their pillow.

# Organic

## 57.

He'd bought the tickets two days before. He'd put them somewhere safe, he was sure. Now though he can't find them anywhere, everything's whirling around him, in ten minutes they have to leave, in half an hour they have to be at Larissis Station, and he's still in the middle of the living-room, unshaven, unwashed, completely lost. He hasn't even packed his things. He throws a few T-shirts into a travel bag and tells her it's time to leave. They can buy new tickets on the spot. On leaving, he doesn't think to check the jeans he was wearing the previous day, that are together with a pile of crumpled clothes flung on the couch. On the contrary, he anxiously searches the bottom of the travel bag and to his relief finds the holy bottle sticking up like an aroused member. He feels secure. His functions return to their natural state. They race outside to get a taxi, while the tickets peep furtively out of the back pocket of his jeans on the couch. Banging the door shut, he doesn't imagine that when he opens it again, it'll be as if he were crossing the threshold of his life for the second time.

## 58.

The train rolls northwards at a steady speed. The two of them side by side with the Boeotian landscape passing rapidly before them. He feels as if he's whirling in a metal vortex, in a concert of chemical elements that are throbbing in keeping with the mad dance of the laws of Physics. The rails grow longer, the metals make contact with a tinny whistling, with a vibrating friction, chrome everywhere intertwined with steel, centrifugal, centripetal and critical mass in an orgy of reactions, a concert of propensities cutting slantwise through the thin air, that surrenders without resistance. She keeps hold of him throughout the journey, with a feeling of fleetingness flowing through her veins. Starting from the eye of a cyclone is a track in the

shape of a snake that evolves into an unexpected regularity nearer the mountain. The
train, a modern one, straight from the service
yard, with its nickel-plated fittings shining aggressively, takes them high up, to another
station, which he has decided will be the set-
ting for the continuation. Here, the accompaniment will not be as it is now, rapid movement,
internal combustion engines and polite atten-
dants. It will be a landscape from the past, a
station from the previous century; the air will
smell of wood and slowness, time will be sta-
tionary. It will be an organic landscape, where
nothing will be moving except him, slowly, prepared, resolved.

During the journey, he got up four times.
Twice to finish one of the bottles in the toilet
and twice supposedly to order coffee – beers,
that is – which he drank at one go as he passed
through the three carriages separating his seat
from the bar. While draining the beer in the
second carriage, he found himself before a
woman of about fifty-five. Blonde, slender, with
fine features. She stared at him in a motherly
way, full of condescension. He wondered what
she must be thinking about him. It's important
to know what the others with whom you share
the world think about you. After they'd passed
by each other, he turned and watched her as she

walked away. A button at the back of her dress was open. Inside her skin appeared shiny, smooth and real. He felt relief.

# 59.

The house in the village. First, they take a stroll in the garden, then they go on up. With not a little effort he shows her around: the tiny bathroom – hewn into the rock – the pictures with the portraits of his ancestors, the veranda from which he filmed the snowballs with his Super-8, the adjacent plot of land where he threw the empty bottles. In the afternoon he tried to implement what the Chinese call 'doing nothing'. It was impossible, the place was so loaded, so ionized with memories of people who'd passed through his life. Each corner emitted a particular smell, objects took on a different meaning, smoke came out of the fireplace sending coded messages, the chairs gaped insolently as if sneering, the wooden rails with the climbing plants branched off in a crazy whirl, till what was left in the end was a scratch, a false note, and that false note was his memories, his memories as they came into the house carried on the mountain air.

That evening, after finishing the second bottle, he managed to take her to the taverna in the square. He tried at great pains to appear all right. They sat there for two hours barely uttering a word. She, furious, with the anger stored up throughout her body, having made her decision, her final decision; he, with his head lolling and arms folded, was asking himself, asking himself what purpose was served by all that absurdity, what delusion was he about to declare to be his destiny. Sitting opposite them was a sixty-year-old writer, equally the worse for drink. He came to sit with them and they drank together, till his mind couldn't take in any more. Much later, the writer would narrate that evening to him, having strangely retained almost every detail. At around one in the morning, he proposed that they leave. He opened the door and went out into a night in which he gasped for breath out of accumulated weariness.

# 60.

Turmoil; feeling his hands full of insects, a pursuit, an inner whinnying, a moon barely visible. The return and the issues that had to be solved. The village, dark and menacing, trembling like a choppy sea. The water flowing from the

mountain peaks towards the sea in streams running to the right and left of the cobbled street,
running incessantly – runnies the locals call
them – and with it the water from the springs
sweeping along papers, notes, tiny images, a
cross, the label from a bottle, time.

On coming out of the taverna he looked at his
hands and saw that the three fingers of his left
hand had joined together as when making the
sign of the cross. Beside his was the church
with its slate slabs and before him the small
square. A multitude of night insects buzzed
around him. He tripped and almost fell. She
grabbed him and they both sat down in the middle of the square under a large plane tree.

'I'm leaving,' she said.

'You don't understand, all yours, me here...'

'Please go and wash, look at your hands...'

'Your ... When I ... here ... here...' – he
looked at his hands.

'You've cut yourself, can't you see? You should
go and wash it. You need help. I can't go on
any more, I'm leaving.'

'Please, let me explain ... I woke up ... in a
stir ... My hands ... There's a reason ... My
mind ... at risk...'

'We've been over this so many times. Go and
wash yourself.'

He went back to the taverna and summarily
cleaned the blood off his hands. The meat-knife.

Under the table. He took hold of it, clutched it. She mustn't see him. He went outside again.

'Let's go to the station,' he said to her.

# Phobia

## 61.

For many days now he's been talking to her on the phone about the station. He tells her about the stream, how it flows babbling between the rocks, about the small glade, about the greenery, anarchic and harmonious at the same time, about the small sheds that for years now have remained to recall another age, about the rusty rails with time's indelible verdigris, about the special signs and, finally, about the short trip to the bridge which goes from the retaining wall as far as the mountain that is divided in two by the ravine and joined by the construction made by the father of a famous painter in the last century. Now they're walking in that direction. After the taverna, his step is unsteady, he stumbles and only with great effort does he manage to walk down the cobbled street with its appreciable incline. They haven't turned on the lights and the place is pitch black; the sheds look like dark shadows; he can't see the stream, just a gentle babbling can be heard; he feels the dampness biting into his bones and stands there, on the lines, with bloodshot eyes, dizzy, blind, literally despondent, with his breath steamy, his saliva viscous. In the distance he hears the sound of an engine approaching. Even though the tiny train hasn't been running for the last twenty-five years, he considers it entirely natural and takes her with him – she ritually follows behind, accompanying a dance of farewell – in the direction of the whistling. Presently, they arrive at the bridge and he sees it at a distance of three hundred metres, a dark shadow, a moving tower that, gasping, clambers up the mountain; it's shaking all over and makes the metal parts of the bridge vibrate, while he feels all the screws, bolts, supports together in a concert of wavering at the zero point of equilibrium. He holds on to her shoulder. He can see everything clearly before him: the train, the bridge wavering, the taverna, the mountain, the stream. The train approaches, gathering speed on the level ground. He looks at her. Then he sees both of them from up above, embracing on the edge of the bridge, night-time, in a mountain village in central Greece. The tiny tails inside him have begun a wild dance, as if they've been struck by an electric current. Now, he can see the train clearly forty metres away like a steaming moving rock. He turns her face towards his. He kisses her slowly. Then, when the beast has arrived at no more than a breath away, he pushes her into the middle of the track and shuts his eyes.

# 62.

'. . . Summer '76, I'm in a discothèque in Kypseli with a group of school friends. Angheliki, a regular date at the time, had brought a girl from France with her. Also present were two boys. The one, short and fair, writes poems and theatrical sketches, in fact he'd staged one of his own about an anarchist who takes over a school and is killed in the end by the police who storm the place; the other, chubby and brown-haired, is playing the role of an aide and is continually perspiring. Both of them keep Angheliki occupied while I dance with Liz. All around us are posters showing half-naked couples in erotic embraces. Communication takes place with the eyes. She looked first at the poster then at me. Though inexperienced, I immediately get the message.

'At her home, Liz put her hands round my neck, she stared at me with an imploring look and kissed me, and I, perspiring and flustered, carried her to the bed, turning off the light with my shoulder at the same time. In the perfect darkness, I worked like the blind: I recognized the protuberances, I crossed the curves, besieged the invisible hills, felt the wet vegetation and smelled the flora's vapours, till red in the face, with my eyes fixed there where hers ought to be, I manoeuvred our bodies into the position that I imagined would render the symmetry of our love. Like two parts of a machine that have to be placed in the appropriate position in order to fit together, our bodies found that desirable position that led to the awaited click and the captivity was complete. I felt as if I'd been robbed of something that was mine, as if my liberated, proud member had been taken captive, engulfed, and with rapid movements I strove to release that clamp, to prevent her from benumbing me, to stop her swallowing me up. I saw that when I reacted in this way, with such passion, with pronounced eagerness so as not to be inactive, not to be caught sleeping, Liz moaned and seemed to enjoy it, and I came to believe that love was precisely this: insurrection in sobriety, continual movement and investigation in complete darkness...'

# 63.

When he opens them again, he feels as if a whole age has passed. He suddenly feels as if the night has lit up, that he can now see every-thing clearly, the mountain, the rails, the vegeta-tion, everything. He looks down. She's lying in the middle of the tracks, curled up, motionless, and a soft crying merges with the rustling of the leaves and the sound of the waters as they car-ess the mountain with their gentle flowing. He looks towards the station. There's nothing. There's no train, no carriages, nothing. Just her lying on the ground crying and at a distance an old grey-haired dog sleeping. He lifts her up, wipes her eyes and they go back home. Without uttering a word. They sleep in the same bed: an intense, difficult sleep.

In the morning he's awake by seven. Still dizzy from the events of the previous night, he fixes a double Absolut with lemonade. He re-members that she'd told him she would leave that day. When she too woke, he tried, with the last drop of hopelessness that the acceptance of the end brings, to mumble something about being sorry, together with some clumsy words of affection and thin excuses that he didn't be-lieve himself. He felt small, tiny, less than noth-ing. And that's just what he was. She, without even condescending to answer, packed her things in that professionally quick way of people who've had their stomach-full of moving around. Self-disciplined, calm, she refrained from opening up any more issues. She came out with a dignified 'Bye' – kissed him on both cheeks – and left. She'd asked him to call her a taxi but he, fuzzy and ill as he was, confused the numbers – they all began with ninety-six and had five digits and there were so many of them, how was he to find the one for the taxi ... In the end she went herself to the café, found the writer, and he put her into a local taxi shaking his head at the same time, as he'd seen the evil coming from the previous night.

For the rest of the day he sat on the veranda gazing down over the bay. He felt as if someone were making an incision in his breast, then slowly opening his ribs one by one, ritually, like the curtain at the beginning of a play. Then he felt the spotlight falling on him and lighting up all those things inside him that glowed red, blue and golden, to the strains of a melancholy musical finale.

# 64.

'. . . I took the keys one Sunday afternoon. It was the first time that I'd seen the apartment. It was in the centre of town, quite small, not particularly light, but it was mine, exclusively mine. In the light of just one desk lamp, I examined the place: a living-room, a bedroom, a kitchen, a small bathroom, and a hall. Everywhere there was a musty smell, which was not surprising given that the previous tenant, an elderly half-crazy woman, never went out at all. I lay down in the middle of the room and stared at the ceiling. Two or three cockroaches were going round in circles. I reflected that I'd be spending at least the next six years of my life in that place. 1978 was a good year. Political affairs at full, fantastic music – I regularly bought imported albums – boys and girls with a mania for experiences, money – and drink – assured. I got up and went over to the mirror. In the half-light, I saw my figure: thin, not particularly tall, fine profile, good physique at that time. I felt as if a carpet were being laid before me, a red carpet, deep red with gold fringes. Walking on this I'd cross the distance that separates the adolescent from the man and at the other end she'd be waiting for me to crown me king (of her heart?), while lined at either side would be friends and relations who would shower me with flowers and acclamation. Among the crowd I spotted my friend Tony, who I'd known from childhood – his father was American – and I immediately cringed. I saw him waxen, expressionless, clutching a dahlia. He was standing alone, at a safe distance from the others, with eyes full of grievance, that hyperactive rogue, that impulsive captain rowdy. I felt alarmed and something jumped in my heart.

'I was getting up to go when, in that absolute silence, the shrill of the telephone echoed deafeningly. The ringing burst like an announcement in the empty room. I froze and almost certain of what I was about to hear, I lifted the receiver, answering the first of the thousands of calls that I'd receive over the next six years. What I heard confirmed my premonition. All I learned was that it was head-on, he was drunk. There was only one beer in the fridge. I left it . . .'

# Quantum

## 65.

A skull without a nose. That's what he sees when he wakes in the morning. First image; above the divan, fixed on a rusty nail, a copper-green skull, with the characteristic slit in place of the nose and the two holes where the eyes should be. From one of the holes, the right one, hangs a thick, yellow thread that reaches down to the floor. He bends down and pulls it. The skull is dislodged and with a crack falls onto the slate slabs of the floor and smashes. Bits of bone cover the slabs, while on the wall there remains the large nail with its head turned upwards like a hook.

He sits in front of the telephone. Through the

window appears the sea, the headland opposite, the vegetation. He knows that by now she'll be at his home. Naturally, she'll have changed her return ticket. Will she have managed to get one for tomorrow? Or perhaps even for today? Whatever the case, he simply must see her before she leaves. Action – reaction. That's how things change, from the one body to the other, from the one soul to the other. And from the one name to the other. Like two natural systems exchanging energy. His own aeolian energy was scattered to the winds; her kinetic energy took everything and left.

He can't stay there any longer. He feels as if the mountain has mined him, has drained his contents, has sealed his limbs. He has to return to Athens to finish what he began. And to initiate something new. He stares at the room: pots left here and there, clothes on the floor, a shoe on top of the fridge. A mess everywhere. Inside and outside. He goes down and gets his case. In it he throws his books, three huge volumes that naturally he never even opened, piles his clothes higgledy-piggledy, wraps the last bottle. Back again. Back for good.

On the train he examined his reflection in the window. Ostensibly calm, shaven, with sunglasses, he seemed fine. He wondered when the imprint would appear, when the outer signs would appear clearly. How was it possible for a sea to be boiling and for its surface to appear calm and unruffled? Against the joints of the tracks, the wheels beat out a minimalist, mournful symphony for percussion. He removed his glasses. His pupils were dilated as if he'd put belladonna on them. Something in the circle of the iris brought him down to earth. It was a small spot like a wing, like a soft thorn that was flying.

# 66.

He arrived in Athens at midday, in the heart of April. He took a taxi to his house. As he was drawing near, one street before his own, he saw her crossing the road. She didn't notice him. She was wearing jeans and a shirt. Her hair was untidy, her look unusual.

On opening the door he was confronted by the same living-room, the same furniture in its place, with the only sign of her presence the open suitcase in the middle of the room. He went down to the store-room in the basement, to the last hiding place to which it was technically impossible for her to have access, and opened another bottle of vodka. He drank greedily from the bottle and went back upstairs. She'd just come in. She didn't seem surprised, most likely she'd been expecting him. She calmly explained to him that she would be leaving the next day. He said nothing. He simply felt that same fear, the one that for so many years had been residing within him, about to well up. He finally realized that the time had come.

The next morning, he was awake at first light. On opening the bathroom door, he noticed on the wooden frame the marks, the etchings and scratchings. He tried to read – as it was a letter – but he couldn't. All he could make out was a four – the fourth month – and a huge 'A' carved so deeply that it made him wonder where they'd found the strength. He brushed his teeth with his hands shaking and went into the living-room. Sticking out of her case was a half-folded map with large red letters. He went over and in the early morning light read four words: 'London A to Z'.

In two hours' time, she would take her case, map and words and would be gone for ever.

# 67.

Afternoon on the same day. He's been asleep for four hours, extinguishing himself like someone else would a light. In those four hours of sleep, a sleep-delirium, it was as if his life passed in fast-reverse, as if he were playing the film backwards at high speed. The period of despair, the fifteen years of adulthood, passed before him like ninety minutes of vomiting; the five years of post-adolescent ignorance like an hour of continuous perspiring and struggle with the sheets; adolescence rushed by with a disagreeable difficulty in breathing and childhood in absolute silence. When he arrived at his birth, he woke up.

He woke up and saw before him all the people connected with him, all those he wanted to exclude from his life, those he denied because he considered that this adventure was his own affair, an exclusively personal price that only he could pay, because he was who he was, because he was different, because he had to give a meaning to all that, *he had to justify the fact that he existed*. Then he gazed at the wall opposite where an oval mirror was hanging aslant. There, on the glass, on the cold, flat, unknown surface, he perceived a light flashing and after some time he clearly saw an image. He saw the bed, he saw the people's backs, the wardrobe, the books and finally he saw the bedside lamp casting a dim light. After so many years, in that weary, dissipated, resigned countenance, concentrating – with a huge effort, it must be said – all his senses, with a calm joy, one of those joys you only feel once or twice in your life, with the relief you feel when you gaze upon the end of a journey, in this tortured countenance he recognized himself, his very own self, as a consummate being.

# 68.

'...The Terrors of the Almighty have been around & against me – and tho' driven up and down for seven dreadful Days by restless Pain, like a Leopard in a Den, yet the anguish & remorse of Mind was worse than the pain of the whole Body. – O I have had a new world opened to me, in the infinity of my own Spirit! Woe be to me, if this last Warning be not taken...'

– Samuel Taylor Coleridge

The next morning, he woke up with a feeling of unbearable exhaustion together with relief. His organism, accustomed to liquid company, immediately ordered a double with orange. Mentally,

he immediately reacted: no. His organism came
back at him in a split second. His mind again
sounded the sharp one-syllable word. This was
followed by a new proposal and so on. He realized that this would go on for quite some time.
The 'no' hurt, burned his guts, appeared so
weak in contrast to the request, the demand of
all his organs for the invigorating lubrication.
He tried to impose a kind of silence, an immo-
bility, whose implacable power would be in a
position to cancel the need to get up and find
the bottle and gulp at it greedily. He imagined
himself getting closer to the mouth of the bottle,
wiping the neck, swallowing greedy, bitter gulps
of processed alcohol. Then he saw the course of
the liquid in his body, the deadly embrace with
his organs and the final storing – load and cor-
rosion at the same time – in his brain tissue.
Next he again saw his body from a distance,
lying on the bed, motionless, covered with two or
three blankets, and all around him a glistening
aura, an aura entirely of breath. He remained
lying there for hours, sometimes repeating his
refusal, sometimes in deep silence, till within
him arose something like an 'analogy' – that's
the only way he could later describe it – something like a sense of equilibrium and proportion, and he felt his bones bending like metal
and taking on a different inclination. His spine
creaked, his pelvis sat up and it was as if his

optical cavity expanded its black cavern. He looked in front of him. A dark grey pachyderm was roaming round the room; it moved slowly, and as if he were somehow inside its skin, he plunged his eyes into its ancient, untainted blood.

# Rheo

## 69.

'...Two in the morning. Athens 1979. I'm
asleep. The telephone rings. A woman at the
other end of the line says: "I know you're looking for a particular girl. I know what you want.
Don't ask me how. I've heard them speaking
about it, I understand, I can feel your need, I
know what you want. I'll be there in half an
hour." I get up half-dazed, I pour myself a double whisky; I think that I'm dreaming. I recall
the conversation I had just four hours ago with
friends, when I told them that I was looking for
something, something special, something different, that no one can understand; none of my
friends could understand what I meant by "a girl
who would flow like liquid". They immediately

took it to be sexual, though that's not what I meant. I pour another. Before I've had time to finish it, the bell rings. I turn off the lights. I don't want to see. A woman enters. All I can make out is that she's dark, thin, older. She says what I expected her to say, what I wanted her to say. The night is marvellous, magical, it flows as all such nights should flow: endlessly. I don't know anything, I don't want to know, I don't even ask her name, nothing. Two people in the same bed at three in the morning on a winter's night in 1979, having spoken for only five minutes on the phone. In the morning when I wake up, I feel uneasy. She left before daybreak. I still belong to the previous night. I'm living in that night. I am the night. The hours that pass before I see her again seemed to me the most magical thing I'd ever experienced till then. Naturally, when we saw each other again, it was day, she told me her name and everything ended . . .'

## 70.

*Hi,*

*I'm sending you the two photos you asked me for. I think they're very good. As I told you in my previous letter, I'm incredibly disappointed that in the end I didn't see anything of what you'd promised me, at least in the way that you'd presented it. I look back over the previous seven months and all I can see is disaster. I've a heavy load to carry, I have to learn from this affair, to learn not to plunge straight into a relationship at least. Now I'm here alone and I'm trying to find a package holiday in a warm country, to go somewhere alone again, though last year I swore I'd never do it again. Try to be well and think how stupid you were to let things end like this. I should never have come in the beginning. I can't help thinking how much this business with you has cost me, even though one more drop of knowledge has dripped inside me. How many more catastrophic experiences before I acquire a little more wisdom and inner strength, till I can at last say 'That's enough!' and start to concentrate on the endless years of inner pain, on the lack of love and support? No more emotional mountain-climbing, I've had enough for several lifetimes. Now I want a few basic things that I've been missing, so simple, so basic and yet so distant.*

    *So long,*

*Z.*

## 71.

Morning, Holy Saturday. At the summer house of a family friend, a split-level house built on the edge of a cliff – the whole sea below. He's come for five days with relatives and friends, twelve people all together. In an unfamiliar state, as if having to learn everything from the beginning: to learn how to speak while listening to the other – an end to the raving monologues – to use his mother tongue properly – avoiding vagueness and the tendency for superlatives – to enjoy silence – and not to rupture it with word-incisions – to maintain some basic order in his living area – and not to scatter everything around him – to eat at a slower rate – and not in bed – to dress with taste – not to wear just whatever resembles clothing – to walk better – with a straight back – and, above all, to sleep better – and not in fits, between nightmares. Still at the stage of adjusting, he's not stopped having those pains in the stomach, in the oesophagus and the spleen, traces of that relentless steamroller. He's still terribly cautious, afraid of exposing himself, he's barely stretched out his leg to wet the tips of his toes in the cold water.

It's ten in the morning, all the others are asleep. He gets up with an uncommon sense of well-being. After a quick cup of coffee, he goes down to the small beach. It's deserted. It's quite a chilly day; a discreet cool breeze warns him about the temperature of the water. As if in a hurry, he throws off all his clothes and plunges naked into the cold font. With vigorous strokes so as not to freeze, he swims out to sea. He doesn't think, he simply distances himself from the shore with the movements of an intrepid swimmer, despite the cold and the slight waves. When he is far enough out, he stops and looks back. He sees the shore, sees the three large leafy trees, the cars of the others parked a little higher up and the house, like a swallow's nest, perched on the edge of the cliff. A sun, still timid, fondles the landscape. Total silence prevails. Further out to sea, a fishing boat slowly plies its course. Beside the left-hand tree, a slender young girl draws water in a bucket from the well. The wind tangles her hair. Everything is as it should be, *in proportion*. He's no longer cold. The day *flows*. With slower strokes, he begins to swim back to shore, in order to dress and get back to the house to say good morning to the others.

## 72.

'...I awake from my afternoon siesta. Peaceful sleep, without dreams. It's hot. Through the window I see the trees in the park opposite. I get up to make a coffee. I walk down a long narrow white corridor with a mosaic floor. Total silence.

At the end of the corridor on the right is the dining-room. Suddenly from inside comes the overture of an opera. The voice of Callas fills the building. On the left, large windows overlook the back part of the well-stocked garden. Someone is mopping the floor with slow movements. Walking down the corridor, I pass by two open doors on my right. Through the first one I see an old woman slowly combing her long white hair. Another woman, much younger, squatting on her bed, is doing a jigsaw-puzzle. Through the second door I see a naked man staring at the floor as if dazed. He doesn't pay any attention to me. As I get nearer to the dining-room, the opera can be heard louder and louder. The image of the diva comes clearly into my mind. She smiles at me. I go into the dining-room. On the television, a dozen or so pathetic local beauties are modelling bathing costumes beside a swimming pool. Callas, a magic carpet, echoes like a dream. I open the fridge and fill the coffee-maker with water. I drink it black . . .'

# Scenes

## 73.

Three months went by. The time flowed like liquid. It passed through ravines, drains, over roadways, over all kinds of surfaces. It was as if he were observing the liquid through the lens of a camera as it crossed expanses, familiar expanses, places that he'd stayed and recalled, and other places too, stored deeper in his memory. As his gaze followed the flow, he saw various objects parading through the transparent liquid: old Byzantine icons, a bicycle wheel, a knife, a seventeenth-century book, a candlestick, photos and mirrors, fragments of broken mirrors. Then, looking through the window, he saw a creeper climbing up and spreading at the same speed as the new blood was flowing in his veins, at the same speed as his bones were reappearing through the skin on his face.

Now it was he that had to cross the flow, to go against the strong current, to navigate the torrent, clutching the letters, with the capital 'A' on top, the damp letters, to get them to the other bank, to save them. And then to dry them and set them out in the right order, after first making the ground firm so they would stand without being rocked back and forth by the wind. And afterwards to stand at a good distance and watch them balancing, some with slanting lines, some with horizontal ones, others with curved ones, some fashioned out of stone, some out of wood, and to watch them standing in a line and to see their shadow, a silent escort, spreading over the moist ground.

## 74.

'...My dreams speak after midnight. All the white of the heart has gone to sleep. Only a black worm swims. Wicker chairs and the brilliant white room creaking. A red head – of a kouros I think – in the middle, with curls and smiling. A cow like a white meteorite, with oriental eyes, sad, and ruminating. When I was small, I drew the constellations. I made them all enormous; so I could touch them. Jupiter blue, the moon red. That's what I did. When, three years old, I saw for the first time from the open car five letters in a row and I realized that the image was a word – 'B-R-E-A-D' – my life began to roll backwards. I beheaded the future to draw on the past. If those regrets, the five winds blowing together, the summers, the come-down, if those blazing two days, if the shades of the others around me were extinguished, who would I be? When the sediment thickens, how horrid is what remains inside! You want to drink water and you drink blood. I think of the knights with their silk garments and swords. How envious I was! Ivanhoe, Sir Lancelot, palaces, velvet, living myths. And then topics for high school essays such as '...The employees wilt at their desks...' and '...Describe Saporta's School Bag...' and I remember. I remember that not one woman ever left her mark on me. Only insects came and went in the vessels. Those that shine and creak like old furniture. We built houses with buckets and mud and our nails smelled of concrete. Coins had sprouted on the branches and I'd steal them. Stars in pairs called to me, and there I was: King Arthur, the Holy Grail and names, names of thousands of knights and places. Walter Scott, the Odyssey, the Titans and Cyclops, Easter

Island, Tierra del Fuego. And then in a dream I heard three drums sounding and I felt something falling from above, something rocky, of an indefinite shape, and I felt it falling inside me, being swallowed, spreading indiscriminately throughout my body's liquids and becoming one with them and it stared at me from within my blood and it has a name that begins with 'A' and then has a 'B' and an 'S' and 'N' and 'T' giving ... Absnt ... Absinthe. I wake from an intense dream. I must be wet through...'

# 75.

Now he was able to work again. Before he'd sit at his desk and for half an hour would remain motionless unable to make the first movement, with his mind reproducing the next five hours as if it were some terrible coercion, counting the hours, the minutes, the seconds. Still three hours and sixteen minutes, still two hours and twenty-seven minutes, one hour and thirty-three ... Now he plunged head-first. He'd begun to realize that the whole secret was there. When he allowed himself to *continue* in some activity, then he actually felt that he was involved in life, that he could escape from his continual self-observation and experience the present with some degree of satisfaction. Reasoning of the type: 'Look at me now how I'm moving the chair, how I'm opening the drawer and taking out the blank paper, now I'm taking the pen and I'll begin to write, I'll finish the page, but then I'll most likely need, a book that's in the living-room, so I'll get up and then perhaps I'll be thirsty and I'll go to the fridge, I may even put on a CD and if I do, what music will I want to hear then, and afterwards I'll probably return to a new page and this will go on until seven and then what's going to happen this evening?' Such fanciful delirium, such an orgy of emotional speculation, had irrevocably passed.

# 76.

'...At home. The seventh anniversary of the Polytechnic School student revolt against the Junta. I've just come back from classes and I'm arranging my notes when the doorbell rings. It's one of my student friends, with whom I do my assignments. I pour out two ouzos, then another two. We talk about what we've been doing, about girls, about politics. After half an hour, the doorbell rings again. I guy I'd met blind drunk at Lookie's the previous night. I vaguely remember his face – a greasy, round face, inquisitive eyes.

He'd run into two girls he knew in the square, did I want him to call them over? I agree, my fellow student approves and before long there we are, the five of us, around a bottle of ouzo. The one girl is thin, pale, sweet, with a fugitive look, in a continually nervy state. She arouses in me an almost paternal feeling, I get the impression that she's ready to burst into tears. The other, loud and plumpish, disappears after a while and comes back with a tall, bony guy, with an angular face and huge green eyes. In the course of the evening, the student and friend go, leaving the two girls and angle-face. He's got onto the brandy, downing it like water. We hit it off immediately, our most wounded lakes unite through the tributaries of alcohol. Our depths are common ones, the same ground that's become wet. There's a distribution of couples and the night passes erotically and unexpectedly. The thin girl is sensual, relaxed and reserved at the same time. In the morning, she unexpectedly goes back into her shell, forming a defensive female alliance with her friend. The light of day has an effect on the bodies. The curves once again become straight, gazes lose their evening moisture. I need a walk. I go out with angle-face and we head for the Exarchia district. On the day after the Polytechnic School anniversary, Athens looks like a town that's been bombed. Broken shop windows, burned cars, a smell of smoke and blood. Virtually no one on the streets. Two people were killed during the previous night as I later learned. Their names began with "K". At one point, two coppers stopped us to check our identity cards. Fortunately, we had them with us. "How old are you?" angle-face asked me. "Twenty," I answered and kicked a half-broken bottle thinking of the thin girl waiting for me at home...'

# Fourth photograph

'Yes, it was worse than I'd imagined. I had to deal with a madman, someone sick. I couldn't stay even one hour longer.'

'I told you. There are people who know only one thing: how to take. He had nothing to give. He was incapable. I saw it from the very first moment.'

'That's not it though. The willingness was there. He had substance, he had reserves. And that was the worst. It's terrible to have to watch someone with his gifts cracking up, fading in front of you. On the one hand he was destroying himself and on the other he made out that nothing was happening. He was playing a game with his own self. Now he's changed again, he's

full of remorse. He sent me a letter so apolo-
getic, so moving that you'd think it wasn't the
same person I'd seen in Athens and in the
mountains. He even remembered to continue
the fun with the photos. Take a look.'

'Looks very formal to me here.'

'He looks like he's coming from some event,
something like a reception given in his honour,
something that, judging from appearances, he
finds particularly unpleasant. Look, here he's at
the same table with all those other people, sitting in the middle as if he's the guest of honour at some official celebration; though he
seems to be elsewhere, to be suffering, his face
is like a mask of pain, it's an ordeal for him to
be there. At the same time he's making a
touching effort to conceal it, but it's impossible,
he's the sort of person who can't hide anything,
everything appears plain on his face. It must be
'92 or '93.'

'Who are they all?'

'I don't know. He seems out of place though,
doesn't he?' He has a look of despair, I can feel
him wishing he were far away, at home, drinking. Why has he sent me this photo, I wonder?
It's as if he wanted to tell me something.'

'Don't dwell on it, little sis. Don't even think
about it. My advice to you is don't ever set foot
in that crummy country again.'

'You don't understand, Bessie. I've got certain

ties there. As for him ... I never want to see him again, though I can't stop thinking of him. In his last letter he told me that he's at the first stage of an important change; that he's stopped drinking – something I can't believe – that he's finally reached the point he needed to begin his "reconstruction" as he puts it. And even if I were to accept what he says, I don't see why you have to reach such depths in order to begin to sort yourself out. He also said something that made an impression on me. He says that a swimmer beginning with backstroke in the two-hundred metre medley is alerted that he's approaching the fifty-metre turn, before reaching it, by a series of coloured flags hanging above him a few metres before the finish, as he doesn't have any visual contact with the finish because of his position. That's how he knows when to prepare his body to make the underwater somersault in order to continue the race using a different stroke. I was for him, he says, the flags that told him when it was the right time for the somersault, for his turning to the next, orthodox style of swimming.'

'I for one don't understand all that. I can see though that you're still thinking of him.'

'Whatever I say, I can't get him out of my mind. Naturally, I don't want to see or speak to him again. I don't know if I'll ever ... And then there's the island itself. There's something about that island, a magnetism, an attraction . . . I can't do without it.'

'So you'll go again!'

'To the island? Yes. I'll take my books, I'll stay in a place away from the harbour, with a girl I know who's an artist, I'll read and swim. I need it. This year was a nightmare. Who knows when I'll be able to relax a bit, to find something of what I'm looking for. I know what I want now. No more difficult relationships. I've finished with them. I'll find some clients for private lessons, I'll save some money and I'll go over to the island for a couple of weeks. As for next year, I can see myself not staying in Europe. I've got something in mind.'

'Are you going to tell me?'

'Not yet, Bessie, wait a bit. Not yet.'

# Therapy

## 77.

Midday on deck, the sun directly overhead and sea, everywhere sea, sea and gulls, all azure and white. In his head he again feels the trembling of those tiny tails, as Mitya called them. But now it's precisely this attribute of theirs, that makes them vibrate, remember and then tremble, that appeals to him. He plunges enjoyably into his memory, swims in time past with the strokes of an Olympic champion, at times diving superbly to bring up something submerged, at others, turning onto his back, and with his arms outspread, hovering between the sun and the surface of the water.

He sees everything differently now. Before

him the chance image constitutes the sum of the individual objects. The boat is a boat, the life-belt a life-belt, the Dutch girl's smile a clear come-on, the people walking on deck his natural extension, a friendly cocoon wrapped around him. He's at last discovered the path of his life, of his time. He walks along it sometimes slowly, sometimes quickly, sometimes stopping and studying the elements he finds on the way. He turns over the stones to see what's hidden underneath – that unexpected greenery – he examines the vegetation, with curiosity he observes the tiny representatives of the animal kingdom that he encounters. Now there's a final destination, he reflects and immediately he hesitates. And if there is no final destination, it's an approach at least, a path towards *something*.

He looks at his watch. 4.44 p.m., 4.7.96. Fours again. Identical equations amid the pulse of the day. I'm travelling, he reflects.

# 78.

He's once again on his island. Late, at around twelve, he watches from his balcony the movement in the small harbour. Three men in front of the nearby bar unload crates of beer. Another man from the place opposite shouts to them. He turns and looks at him. It's the well-built Frenchman, the one he'd met last year on the boat. Their eyes meet. Before Jacques can get out as much as a 'Hi', he goes quickly back into his room. A bad omen, he thinks.

He dresses, gets ready and, scrutinizing his appearance, he approves of his clear gaze, the steady hand, the absence of any inner trembling, his slim body. While going down the steps, he compares this natural process of going out with the ritual of the past, the desperate gulps, the anxiety, the surrounding fear. He goes out wearing a white shirt, black jeans and his self.

He's already been sitting for an hour in the club, engrossed in the futile exchange of glances with any number of good-time girls who, having given their everything on the dance floor, will go home to sleep alone or, at best, with some patient – though exhausted – guy who sits it out till the morning. The libido is consumed in the non-stop swaying to the throbbing sounds of a repetitive music usually without words – the constant refrain: 'Freed from desire, my own senses purified'. He tries to determine the kind. The only thing that comes to mind is something like work music, cable music, a fabricated cyber-sound or some such thing at any rate. On the dance-floor a swarthy character, most likely an Arab, is dancing at a frenzied rhythm. His partner is a girl in a mini-skirt – he sees her from behind. Her movements have a familiar look, the bending of the knees, the slight tilt of the head, the tossing of her hair backwards. He focuses his attention to her. Suddenly, she turns towards him. He recognizes her straight away, it's her, a little fatter, with a different hairstyle and, so it seemed, with a new boyfriend. For a brief moment of time, a few seconds, he fixes his gaze on her and the previous ten months pass like an express train through his mind. At some point, he loses her from his vision only to discover her again almost immediately half-hidden behind a huge speaker. She's spotted him and is hiding from him playfully, like a little girl. He gets up, goes over to her and greets her. Somewhat embarrassed, she tells him that she knew he was on the island, but that she didn't want to see him or speak to him again. 'All right, I won't bother you, then,' he answers and starts to walk away. Z. grabs him by the arm and shouting in his ear – since the noise in the place was deafening – says to him: 'As we've met like this, let's have a drink together tomorrow at eight.' The swarthy guy buts into the conversation; he's from Egypt, a fisherman by the name of Hosni. He's well-built, wearing a striped T-shirt and his eyes are as black as coal.

He speaks a little broken Greek, no English or German.

How do they communicate, he wonders, what language do their bodies speak, how can incomprehensible languages run through people's bodies? That was his mistake from the beginning, that he didn't communicate with her in language; whatever he managed to convey to her was only through the body, through the body which is itself a form of language, a language with rules, with syntax, with verbs and subjects, with pauses. Just like language, so the body too is unable to say everything, it can't speak the whole truth, it can't speak literally.

He got up and left, while behind him music dripped like dead stone.

## 79.

At half-past eight he was sitting outside Lina's bar, which was closed this year. She hasn't come yet – but he expected that. He wondered why she'd played the game of hide and seek with him the previous evening. There's no doubt that the seven months that their relationship had lasted with the continuous trips back and forth, with the unbearable daily routine, with their love at extreme temperatures, with their bodies huddled together, perspiring with fear and longing, are not things easily forgotten. Just as the investment, the patience, the straining of nerves and the refutation are not easily forgotten. She would never understand who he really was. It was not surprising given the way he'd presented himself to her, as the last 'iceman'. Their meeting had begun with the best possible omens, with the cleaned-up biographical background and the clever marketing with which he'd tried to promote himself, before, that is, the image gradually began to blur, the tree to shed its leaves, till all that remained was a skeleton full of pain, white bones that creaked in the double bed. And yet she was the only woman in many years, perhaps the only one in his life, who'd managed to scratch even the surface of his flesh, who'd found warmth in his soul's liquids, the evaporating liquids of his anxiety.

A quarter to nine and there she was, with her extra kilos, with her five-foot-seven in all its magnificence, her hair shorter, red blouse, short black skirt, canvas shoes, scarf, rouge, eyeshadow, saying in the same soft voice – perhaps a tone higher to emphasize the required distance in view of the new circumstances – that she was sorry, she'd been held up at a friend's and so on.

They went to a taverna by the sea, ate crab and salad, she drank wine, he lemonade. 'So at long last you've taken me out for once like a man ought to do for his girlfriend. But why do you have to do everything when the party's over?' She explained to him that she didn't want to see him, as she thought that he would have demands, that he'd want them to be together again, that she couldn't, she'd been frightened, she'd invested so much and found herself caught up in madness, in an insanity, that nothing like that had ever happened to her before and so on. He told her calmly that he didn't have any demands, that the steamroller had to pass over him, so it seems, to clear away his congealed anxiety, so he could change his skin, free himself from that black hide that was suffocating him.

She listened attentively and appeared to agree. Inside she didn't believe a word.

# 80.

She didn't believe a word because inside she'd dried up. She was convinced that apart from his egocentrism, his incompatibility and his dependence, there were important differences, differences of a kind that couldn't be bridged. At the same time, however, she also recognized some similarities, for example, that both of them were 'original', idiosyncratic characters, they both had a goal in their lives – even though his was still somewhat obscure – they both required a lot of love and freedom to move, their motives were particularly strong, they both wanted to leave some kind of mark, a trace of their passing, they both had a problem of co-existence with the 'outside' world, they had conventional and unconventional sides, they were composite personalities and they both had problems with their health, on a completely different level, of course – here she shuddered when she recalled how sarcastically he dismissed her inexplicable bouts of sweating, her permanent affliction with 'flu symptoms, her allergy to certain foods and how the expressions 'environmental illness' and 'alternative medicine' left him coldly indifferent.

On the other hand, of course, the differences between them were enormous. She was much better at conversing with the 'outside' world, he had only just begun to make contact with it; she actually concerned herself with others, she took an interest in those around her, he was shut up in the tower of his Ego; she came from a social environment in which she herself meant nothing, she had to fight hard in order to exist, so they'd notice her, he was always the misunderstood centre of his surroundings; he'd been flattered, accepted, while she had been trodden on, virtually broken. This comparison seemed so unjust to her; on the one hand she felt enmity that, while he hadn't been there for her in her ordeal, he nevertheless demanded special treatment, and on the other, she felt sorry for him and couldn't understand why – given that his problems seemed to her to be more manageable – he'd let himself slip into that state.

The waiter brought her back to reality. She started to take out her money, but to her great surprise, he paid for everything. He's doing it for show, she thought.

# Utopia

## 81.

After the meal, their paths parted. He had a date with a Swedish girl – he'd met her at the house where he was staying, she was renting the room next door, without balcony but with a huge window that covered the entire wall and brought the stars of the Aegean night straight into her bed, so she slept beneath a starry vault – she had a date with Hosni, the Egyptian. However, their parting proved to be shortlived as they'd arranged their dates at the same club, the two-storey building with the nice, nostalgic music, Pretenders, Eurythmics, J.J. Cale. And there they were, sitting side by side with their drinks, she vodka and orange, he non-alcoholic fruit punch, at one in the morning, in the middle of

a clear, warm night in June, not having seen
each other for three months – she remembering
a wounded animal, afflicted in bed, he white
walls and worry beads of bone – waiting for a
Swedish shop-assistant and an Egyptian fisherman in order to spend the night, a night that was
divided into two, like their mood, into the 'outer'
night, with its polite behaviour, the small affected movements, the roundness of expression,
and the 'inner' night, that which was infiltrating
deeper and deeper into inaccessible vessels and
smelled as every 'inner' night smells: of fear.

# 82.

'. . . Spring of '84, I'm working at home with a
fellow student on an assignment. It's a semester
assignment, very important – we have an original approach to the subject, it'll create quite a
stir a few months later. It's midday, I've already
started on the ouzo, he doesn't drink, he stares
at me with a look of disgusted condescension,
though I sense that somewhere inside is a latent
admiration of the type "He lives free like that
and at the same time he's a good student and
stands out and he lives alone and has various
girlfriends and he's always going on trips, how
does he do it?" and so on. At around two, the

doorbell rings. It's a friend, five years older than me, just back from France where he was studying. He was passing through my neighbourhood with a girl he knew and thought he'd drop in for a coffee. The girl is hidden behind an enormous sandwich. In place of an introduction, without saying a word, I grab her by the arm and take a huge bite. Nonplussed, she mumbles her name: Leto. "Come in, make yourself at home," I answer, while together with the soft, spicy taste conveyed by the morsels of sandwich, another one, infinitely stronger, descends into my guts and stirs them.

'Thirteen hours later and after having spent the whole day together – my fellow student took to his heels straight away and the assignment was postponed indefinitely – and after having met with a crowd of people – my friends and her friends – at various haunts in the city, I return home alone after a promising and allusively articulated "Goodnight", that by no means suffices me. As soon as I enter my house, I phone her and in response to her initial and justifiable surprise, as it's been no more than a few minutes since we left each other, I retort with resolve, helped by a generous quantity of alcohol that I've consumed during the course of the day: "I'm coming over to your place. Both of us know that's what we want."

'Our night is a glittering one, full of red, gold and blue colour and floods of refreshing waters that surge forward *en masse*, to recede into a calm and embarrassed morning that will later draw the two of us to the easternmost point of the continent, to what the English call Land's End, to a utopia that lasted as long as those breaks in reality...'

# 83.

With his sandal he touched the wooden deck of the boat. A sound of creaking, a swaying bordering on stumbling made him speed up the next step, jumping over the strewn crates used for collecting the catch of fish, over the legs of his fellow-travellers, some crossed, others stretched out, others pale – then he looked up and risked a precarious equilibrium in the hope of a promising look – and others sunburned, eventually finding temporary refuge next to the engine. He was only just in time; the boat set off immediately. Its destination was the familiar small beach. He reckoned that most of the passengers would get off at the one before, a noisy, organized beach with water sports, a bar and umbrellas. He preferred the distant and, if possible, completely deserted ones. He'd taken two books with him, *The Moor's Last Sigh*, by Rushdie and the *Livro do Desassossego* by Pessoa, that he read alternately, leaping from one to the other at such a speed that the painter, Aurora Zogoyby, and the employee, Bernardo Soares had begun to enter into each other's world and the two books, though miles apart from the point of view of content, narrative technique and style, had begun to intertwine and converse – in fact, he'd imagined the heroes meeting, falling in love and living to a ripe old age; the employee developing into a famous philosopher and exponent of the theory of the inner plane and she into a medical researcher with two Nobel Prizes – for Medicine and Peace – to her credit. He stretched out full, took off his sunglasses and, closing his eyes, sank into a bath of sun to the accompaniment of the gentle rocking of the boat.

On arriving on the shore, he saw that only two other passengers had remained. The boat tied up alongside a small jetty and he allowed his eyes to roam around. There were two or three groups of nude bathers scattered over the beach and a single girl, lying face down, also nude. This time he recognized her immediately. With an even suntan, with her body in a position that was a combination of carefreeness and erotic provocation, as if she knew that someone was watching her. As he went to step out of the boat, she stood up and their eyes met. He felt a sense of suspension, as if he were in the middle of a theatrical pause, as if time had suddenly stopped and he had been immobilized with one foot on the edge of the boat and the other barely touching the rock, holding the two books in his hands – the Moor and the wet streets of Lisbon – his bag in the other – containing only a litre of mineral water – and with his eyes fixed on hers (*more steadily and yet so uncertainly*). He turned round on the spot and went back, making up his mind to leave the island as soon as possible.


# 84.

'. . . I saw that I was hanging high in the firmament, as if I were reverently holding on to the sky's hooks and was suspended amidst thousands of stars, with my own weight, with my feet encircled by winged straps, my entire self a heavenly body, and suddenly I let myself go with a jolt and I fell and felt a force that was still not gravity; it was a different kind of force, a magnetic force, that was pulling me and directing me downwards, and the atmospheres and colours and light changed around me, I passed from dark blue to purple and from orange to pale yellow, and I felt first hot then cold, with the light alternating with the darkness and the absolute void, while I tried to clutch hold of something solid, but to no avail, as I continued to fall at a breathtaking speed and felt a sensation of red, which marks the passage from tranquillity to terror, a sensation that the landscapes were changing, that the galaxies were whirling, that I could hear a drumming sound growing louder, till the second jolt came and I realized I'd entered the atmosphere, and there it was as if things settled down: I fell with less speed and passed through the clouds, I touched the dawn as if it were beside me, I found myself bathed in a refreshing rainbow, I smelled the familiar air and, as I came nearer, at some distance below, I saw a flock of birds but I didn't have time to discern what kind of birds they were as the enormous force was pulling me downwards, till I felt a third jolt, more intense than the others, and I perceived another element that I had entered and everything at once turned dark and absolute quietness filled my soul and body, as I continued to descend at a slower rate and to feel cold in a crystalline coldness, until gradually the landscape began again to open and I saw shoals of large fish and strange plants full of shells and vast caverns gaping at me, with all their eyes a stone, and an

eerie deep blue coming to dye them with force,
till I felt my feet touch – strike more like –
something that seemed like ground and I felt
cold and couldn't see properly and following the
impact it was as if the ground was like taut skin
and I bounced and felt a new thrust upwards
and began to make the journey in reverse, now
knowing the route though, I was prepared for
every change and it was as if my body had now
become accustomed and I let myself watch without fear and then I saw beside me the elephant
flapping its ears like a ray and I passed it by
and wondered when I'd again arrive on high so
as to hang on tight this time, and not fall
again...'

# Valve

## 85.

The summer was now coming to an end and he'd remained alone in the city. He was feeling much better, but there were still those flutter-ings, the pricking in the chest, to remind him of the Big Chills. He tidied up his home, spent a whole weekend cleaning it, threw out a pile of old things, clothes, photos, letters, painted the bedroom, rewrote his list of telephone numbers, removing the names of those he no longer wanted to see, began a diet, enrolled in a gymna-sium, set out an ambitious work programme for the new season, began to write a journal, took care of the latest legal loose ends that had in-truded in his life, bought a new computer, re-solved to go again to the films he'd seen during the previous season but couldn't remember and stuck on the fridge door a passage from a book he'd recently read: 'We're so taken up with the adulteration of our feelings, we've made such an abuse of the microscope to study the disgusting growths and the horrible moles that cover our hearts, that we're unable to speak the language of other people. How much better were those times when our souls didn't think, but simply lived and rejoiced!'

# 86.

'...At a party some ten years before. I'm the host, I'm living abroad, towards the end of my studies. A friend and I have invited around one hundred people into an area of sixty square metres. While getting the place ready before the people arrived, I thought of that girl, Danae, who I'd invited at the last moment just three days before. I was sure that something would happen that night between us. In the very few words that we'd exchanged, there was that right mix of aggressiveness and interest, distance and complicity. When patrolling the forest of acquaintances, my intuition, in full bloom then, had smelled a fire starting to flare in her bower. The party was a huge success. At least that's what the others told me, as I spent the entire night with her and a bottle of Absolut.

'The next day dawned like the beginning of a voyage of discovery, a voyage between us, with a common wind blowing without direction, a wind that lasted a number of years, quite a few more than it should have. I woke up first and gazed at her while she was sleeping. Her youth, sweetly lying on the duvet, was a perfect match for the room, the mirror, the furniture, and me.

'The apartment was on the first floor; it over-looked a park full of greenery. There was total quiet; cars passed only every half hour. I got up, made her a coffee; she woke gently, with a slow cat-like rhythm. Her night-dress suited her, she wasn't made-up and she looked even better than she had the previous night. She had a tiny mole on her navel and a tattoo on her right hip. It depicted a snake, most probably a boa constric-tor, that was eating its own tail. Eight years later, the day that she telephoned my place and I wasn't the one to answer, she got rid of it. Removing it hurt a lot, much more than having it done, she'd said then...'

# 87.

He went out into the city streets very late at night – it must have been around four in the morning – and recalled his secret life, the one he lived beneath reality, and he remembered how difficult it was for him to buy the bottles from the supermarket out of fear that they'd notice him, that they'd point him out, and he remembered how he'd stand silent in front of the assistant, with the expression of one frozen, motionless, with the notes in his hand, looking now at the bottles now at the notes with the assistant thinking that he was a deaf-mute because of his dumbness, because of his indecision. And the assistant would ask 'is that what you want?' and he'd nod a 'yes', quickly handing over the money, waiting with unbearable discomfort while the bottles were being wrapped – he always preferred it to seem that they were for a gift; and then the added anxiety of finding a new supermarket, another off-license, so as not to be stigmatized as the one coming in for two bottles every day ... Fortunately, there are lots of places that sell alcohol in the neighbourhood, he's made a list and he goes to each one in turn, so that the amounts he buys will seem reasonable to each assistant. How stupid that he still cares what others think, how he appears to the assistant, to whoever; what a lie, what a monstrous lie, what a daily death his life was! How could such an innocent, colourless liquid have such power! On a few rare occasions he reflected on it and, drinking water, he imagined it mixed with alcohol and pretended that he was getting drunk. Once he even thought that he'd managed it and had gone out of the house blind drunk, singing and dancing, till he dried out and went back to drink the real stuff.

Now he was walking through the city at daybreak and recalling the days that he left behind him a trail of blood like a wounded animal. His breath, acrid and disgusting, surrounded him like a cloud, the vapours of a creature in a state of decomposition, a chemical substance breaking up. He felt then that flowing through his valves was a filthy substance, full of impurities, while a platoon of hungry beggars in ragged clothes was patrolling throughout his body, cursing each time the valve changed direction and vomiting over every organ that they encountered on their path.

Outside, as he walked, he saw only people. People everywhere, neither houses nor objects, only people, outside only people, people and other people, even more, thousands, but no answer from anywhere.

# 88.

Since returning from the island, he'd thought of her often. He remembered what she'd said to him about how we can increase the frequency of the positive occurrences in our lives, how we can 'lift' every person that enters our energy field; how many opportunities we waste in our lives because we don't attach any importance to a friendly observation because we don't have our eyes open; how, while in the beginning we have our questionings, later it's our dreams, coincidences and intuitions that provide us with the answers, answers that are to be found in wrapped packages discarded at the side of us, waiting for us to unwrap them. 'We have to be tuned in to ourselves,' she told him, 'follow our presentiments, be on the alert, because the messages come from all directions and we allow them to pass us by.' He rejected all this with a sarcastic smirk. It sounded like an oxymoron, but he who lived his life in a whirl, as if in a dream, who concentrated only on the problem of existence and the intellect, seemed in theory to be the most realistic, the most materialistic.

He wondered how he had organized his thoughts all those years. What were his views on the great questions in life, what were his ambitions, what was his opinion of himself? He recalled that very often he looked at himself in the mirror and he could find no correspondence between the sum of the features that he saw and what he actually was. Now that he was looking, he knew that that oval imprint was called a face and that it was his image in the world.

# Wysiwyg

## 89.

The plane is a small one, just eighteen seats. The journey to the island in the Sporades was short, just forty minutes. He sits in a seat that makes him think of the local buses. Everything begins creaking before they're even ready for take-off. Beside him is a dark-haired girl, foreign, around thirty. Very thin, tall, dressed in black, without make-up. She's reading a book. She appears absorbed – most likely she's afraid of flying at a great height in that old crate and the book is intended as a diversion. As soon as the plane gathers height, a welcome sleepiness spreads throughout his body. He feels particularly relaxed, almost in his element. He reflects that he's going through yet another experience, the flight, for the first time sober. How many times has he travelled in his life by plane? Sixty, seventy? He's not in a position to remember even one; they are all enwrapped in a hazy cloud, or rather in earth, in primeval earth, in turf that covers him like an ancient skeleton. All he remembers from previous flights is that he imagined amazing things happening to him – flirting with the hostesses, assassinations of VIPs, hijackings, mad sex in the toilets, meetings with important people. All public areas, particularly moving ones, vehicles, ships, planes, were for him the ideal ark for fantasies, a stage on which he conceived, played and directed extravagant works with himself always as the leading actor. Up there in the clouds was the ideal surroundings, an untouched, expansive area, the air that's shattered, the condensed vapour, the speed, the engines and the metal, all of which constituted an exceptional décor for the fantasy, which, with the help of alcohol, wove ever more composite narrative forms; forms so complex that his director's weft appeared to be continually suspended in a maelstrom of visions and scenic meanderings, so that the landing always found him exhausted, perspiring and incredibly tired, obliged to continue his reveries in a new, down-to-earth reality.

Now it was different. He was there, he was in

the cabin, he saw real people around him, recognizable people, one-dimensional, and yet once again a new, different bugbear seemed to have gripped him. He recognized the difference. Now it was the persons themselves, the specific faces that drew him into that stimulating wandering. The forms he wove this time were like engravings in stone, with accents, deep incisions of an extraordinary depth. The fragments of stone scattered in the cool wind as he sensed the journey was coming to an end. The girl beside him sat up and closed her book. For an instant their eyes met. Her gaze was direct, penetrating. He lowered his first and just managed to see printed in italicized artistic letters the title of the book: *What You See Is What You Get.*

## 90.

On another island, further north, he knows no one, he knows no one here, all he knows is that he'll stay as long as he likes, he hasn't booked for a fixed number of days, he'll stay as long as he likes, he has money, all he cares about is to have a good time, to let his hair down, one and a half months of misery and shut inside, then there was that whole year of endless sliding, add on the fifteen years that he simply knocked about, and if you reckon that he's still young, then he has some ground to cover, he has time to make up for, many years – lost because of a wrong step, a bad throw of the dice – he wants to make up for lost time, to enjoy himself on that island and to see whether he knows how, if he can adapt to the way others enjoy themselves, if on this island with the pretty harbour – he noticed two nice bars to the left of the jetty – if on this island he can be himself, there, over there, he'd go to those bars on the front, from outside they appear to be to his liking, the first one is dark with wooden panelling on two levels, crammed with people, the barman sprays the stone wall with spirit and then sets it alight, it's one in the morning, in the Olympic Games in Atlanta the Turkish weightlifter has done it again over the Greek Leonidis, afterwards there was an interview with Leonidis' wife – very lovely – and he wondered why they didn't get an interview from the wife of the other Greek champion who talks only of his little daughter and why not about his wife, and he stood there holding his fruit juice, perspiring among the crowd jostling him, and over the speakers came the sound of the 'Macarena' at which five girls got up to dance on the bar and one was very beautiful, dazzlingly beautiful, with legs a mile long and dressed in black, with a predatory look, dark-haired, and he recognized her as the same

girl who had been sitting next to him on the
plane reading and their eyes had met and so on,
and when the 'Macarena' stopped, she went behind the bar – she was a bar-woman in fact –
and once she was back there, something changed about her behaviour, she changed from
being an aggressive female into an obliging hos-
tess, and he went to order yet another fruit juice
and again that gaze, and despite all the people,
despite the dozens of customers pushing and
trying to get to the bar, she ignored them all
and concerned herself only with him and asked
him where he was from – she was Italian –
breaking into a charming grin of surprise when
she learned he was Greek – she'd taken him for
a foreigner, most likely an American, with his
Indian features and cheekbones – though he
didn't know how to take it as he still hadn't
learned how to behave when sober, then she
gave him another five fruit juices on the house,
the orange ran out and it was three in the morning when she drew close to him and whispered
in his ear that she had something to confess to
him, that it was something serious, and he was
surprised, what could be so serious as they'd
only known each other for two hours, and he
urged her to tell him, to be taken aback to hear
her saying that he mustn't think they were
going to make love that evening and to be left
dumbfounded as he'd done absolutely nothing

to make her think such a thing, on the contrary it was she who had given him the drinks and had gone on for so long about Santa Giuliana, the saint that protected her, and about her dreams, how she wanted to be a journalist, and about her former boyfriend, who was the owner of the bar and so on, and who'd ignored all the customers and the hordes of admirers who were pushing and shoving in front of the bar, trying – in vain, it must be said – to get near her, while he was monopolizing – shamelessly so, it seemed – the interest of this astoundingly beautiful bar-woman, and besides it was she who had filled his stomach with such an overdose of vitamin C, capable of keeping him in a state of hyperactivity for two whole days and nights before brimming over and being discharged through his urine – in short, it was she who was pulling the strings, while he, trying to keep some equilibrium in his new role, had adopted a cool, low profile, trying with particular zeal to investigate at first hand those mechanisms governing sober enjoyment, only to be rewarded, shocked, by that unexpected statement, which he was in no position either to evaluate, much less to negotiate.

# 91.

'. . . I wake up in a small house at the foot of the Acropolis. Autumn '93. I get up from a disturbed night's sleep, a night of tossing and turning, that consisted mainly of a fight with the covers. With fear and annoyance, I wrap myself in the thick blanket and curl up still shaking. She's sitting on the bed beside me, coquettish with her straight black hair and her round face, with an aura of television glamour – he'd met her two weeks before. Looking at her I feel my whole body breaking out into a sweat, I feel my pores overflowing with a bitter liquid, tiny bugs patrolling my skin, while at the same time she's smiling at me, provocatively and available, revealing her breast that's small and adolescent, in contrast to the maturity surrounding her eyes. I recall her friend in the taverna the night before leaning over and saying in her ear "he looks like he's just recovered from an illness" and she laughing and explaining to him – scattered words that I picked out with my practised ear in full operation – giving him a summary of everything I'd told her – and I'd told her plenty – that I'd just come out of a heavy relationship, that I wanted to make a new start and so on.

'And now, in the morning, in a strange house, in a familiar state, still without as much as a mouthful, with a woman available and quite presentable, with that humour characteristic of her circle, a mixed kind, a cocktail of Mediterranean bourgeois and provincial affectation, just like those girls who chose to adopt that bastardized coquettishness promoted by our national film-star as a model of behaviour. But okay, things are relaxed; we laugh, and she thinks we have a great time. Of course, I find it inconceivable that she behaves towards me as if I were completely normal, that she imagines that everything we've done, everything I've said, making a tremendous effort to use my body sufficiently, to come out with a respectable conversation, I did without any strain, as if it all came out spontaneously. It's amazing how you can fool the other, even during the most private moments.

'She got up to fix breakfast and I turned over on my face, to squeeze out a little more time for solitude, a little more time for regrouping my forces...'

## 92.

He caught the flying Dolphin to the next island, Skiathos. Verdant, crowded, August mayhem.

What concerned him more than anything else
was to see the house of the island's famous
author. It was closed when he got there so he
sat at a café and ordered herbal tea in his honour – he remembered that it was the author's
favourite drink. Was it he wondered the herbal
tea or the alcohol that sharpened his imagination, was it he wondered the alcohol that in the
middle of his life's furnace garbed him in that
camouflage, that this man of ivory, of silk, never
divested himself of? How, when you emerge
from a dream to return to reality, when behind
your friends' high spirits you see a whole
Bacchic ritual, Love itself in the eyes of your
beloved, the very face of Fear in a sharp stone,
can you once again go into the usual room, exchange the required chit-chat, worry about your
daily needs? With what can your thirst for
dreaming be exchanged? Perhaps only with the
thirst for now. It was along paths such as these
that he wandered while drinking his herbal tea
in the island's main square, opposite the verdant hill with the theatre. He also thought about
returning to Athens the next day; the summer
was ending and a new period beginning, one
that he'd get through without any disguise, but
more or less as he was now, with a T-shirt,
shorts and the distillation of the tea running
carefree through his guts. The author's house
remained shut all afternoon. It might never

open. Perhaps that's how he wanted it, he thought, and headed off towards the ticket office to arrange his return.

# Xenolith

## 93.

He'd often cart around with him an imaginary listener with whom he'd engage in conversations on all manner of topics, particularly during periods of waiting, when he expected some important event to take place, a significant meeting, an appearance in public, a telling phone call usually of an amorous nature. During the period of waiting he felt an inner trembling, and a part of himself, specialized in fictional exercises, attempted to fashion all the possibilities. Now he's on the fourth floor of a huge open-plan complex, with dozens of computers in an Orwellian line, its high-tech style, its blonde secretaries with their long legs and just a suspicion of grey matter, the employees with the outwardly cool style concealing their innate nervousness, and he tries once again to draw his imaginary listener into a thorough investigation of the place, into an analytical breakdown of the environment, so as to clarify his own particular presence, to determine from the start his role in there, namely that he's waiting to see the director and that this is something he's doing for the first time because always in the past matters of work were ready, they were already on a plate, whereas now he's waiting for the director with a pile of papers in his bag, which are products of his ideas, ideas which came to him spontaneously, without him having to concern himself particularly, they came in abundance, *from his inner wealth*, now we'd see how they would appear to the director.

Now, however, his listener is no longer there, he's withdrawn, just as many years before his friend from upstairs had withdrawn, the same one who was responsible for all the mischief he got into as a child. Just as Thomas Chatterton had invented the imaginary Thomas Rowley, a monk from Bristol who lived in the fifteenth century, as the person who wrote his poems, so he too, when he was a little lad, had invented Thomas, who, as a faithful friend, was held responsible for all his pranks and escapades.

So now he was alone, truly alone, with a feeling that he was keen to send from his mind to his central nervous system so it could find expression, but it persisted, wanting to remain there, as if saying no, all that you're thinking has no relation at all with external expressions, they can't cross that threshold, they're matters of the mind and that's where they should stay. For once – a choice that before was extremely rare if not non-existent – he decided to follow the upper control room. This then advised him to remain calm for the remaining half-hour wait, led him to gaze at the neck of the girl on the switchboard, to reflect on the adequacy of the air-conditioning in the open-plan offices and to make a shortlist of the provisions required for his fridge that had been empty for the last few days. He entered the director's office and looked him in the eye.

## 94.

'...On the eve of the big day, I'm unbelievably nervous, we'd decided to spend the evening at home – I don't want to – but nor do I want to go out with the lads as per usual. I pop into the local shop to buy a new cage for the canaries; she's gone to see her parents. We have to work

out our expenses – expenses and canaries and
the tickets for our trip keep us busy for a couple
of hours; I want to go out, I haven't drunk very
much and I need it, my organism needs lubri-
cating, needs inoculating with artificial escape,
and she poor thing is upset, she'd naturally imagined this day differently, as an exceptional, un-
ique date, and now here she is on the eve of her
biggest day looking at me in an excited state,
aggressively, with me swearing at her over the
money, over the canaries, over the tickets, with
me choosing that time – yes, that time and that
day – to talk about important matters, about
time, about love and life, about getting out of
that game, about shaking the foundations of
what we think is our love for each other, to see
what's underneath, and she being confused and
not understanding, believing as she does that
what's being expressed at that moment is in-
deed our love, just as what we're experiencing at
that exact moment is time – that's what she's
always believed, that was always the norm. I tell
her that love is always an illness, at best it in-
volves "wanting" and "possessing", and I ask
her "Do you love me?" and she answers "Very
much" and I see that she really means it and
that hurts me, and I'm saddened by the fact that
I know I'm taking things as far as they'll go, to
the heart of experience, to know that too, to ex-
haust it, to destroy it and to be born again, to

sort things out. What I ask of her is that she be there, to be next to me so I can talk to her, to explain to her, but what I see – no doubt it's my dizziness, my tendency to lubricate things that's to blame – is a woman still without shape, a female pulp calling me to fashion her, to shape her, to fasten her to my right side and breathe life into her. And yet, deep in her eyes I see precisely what I mean, that light possessed by creatures that believe totally, those creatures full of life's affirmation, and I reflect that I'm going to have to drink a lot so as not to remember that, yes, not to remember that day, above all not to remember the next one . . .'

# 95.

The week fell into some sort of order. A flexible timetable, commitments, contacts, successes, social life, new acquaintances. Less frequent letters from her, bits of news, details about work. He answered in the same way, with a few references to the past, to what he was doing, to changes in his life. An underlying grievance and a concealed bitterness, mainly on her part, characterized their correspondence.

One weekend he went on an excursion to

Aegina with a girl, Julie, that he'd only just met.
They sat down on the beach in front of the tem-
ple and she read some of her verses to him:
'Amid the day, amid the light, how the sounds
shine, the breeze blows when calm, I want to be
sounds and light, a continuity that belongs no-
where, a breeze that scatters reality far away.'
He liked that girl with the slight down on her
face, the hair that smelled of grass, verdure or
some such thing, the arched eyebrows and the
shy smile. He liked how she kissed him, how
she opened and closed her lips, like the rising
and falling of the tide, always leaving a fibrous
bridge of saliva to symbolize the distance and
rendering the contact between the two bodies
more bearable. A bridge that with the very next
movement was put under strain and, as it
broke, was distributed equally between their oral
cavities, while her hands, with their long, slender fingers – her thumbnail was ultramarine –
made circular shapes on him, fully co-ordinated
and guided by her youthful muscles, her arteries
and bones, which, condemned by their nature to
rigidity, strove in vain to turn, to encircle his
body in an act of giving that was shamelessly
uninhibited. They spent a whole afternoon talking in a taverna, with the sixteen-year difference
between them separating them like the line of
the horizon, talking about the same things, each
from their own viewpoint, with an overpowering

desire to extract as much as they could from each other. The following morning on the boat, the alternating hues of dawn produced incessant tones of red and, as they watched them from the deck hand in hand, she saw stretches of blooming roses and he, a jet of thick, steaming blood.

# 96.

Writing at home in the afternoon, he makes plans concerning how he wants his life to unfold from that time forward and how he might leave the door half open so no one will be afraid of entering his realm – unknown among unknowns – how he'll allow the light to enter, to diffuse through his life, and as it spreads, to colour the part he'd never allowed – light, true light, not scattered fragments, not strips whose limits he doesn't know how to accommodate, pure light, the whole of which he'll allow to penetrate him, the kind of light that makes dust glisten, light like a filter covering the cool air – and open, illumined like that, his form will acquire a look of seriousness under that glow, as it bathes and breathes in it, and life will unfold as if from a shining spout.

The telephone rings. It's her. She's calling him from Germany. She's leaving, she tells him, the next day for Israel on the eight-thirty flight. She's attending a conference and she'll have one day free in Athens. Could she come by the house and spend the day with him? If it wouldn't be any bother to him, and so on.

At seven-thirty in the morning, he's sleeping soundly, the doorbell rings. He opens, not like in the past, but in the calm of a rewarding sleep, in the intermission in a dream. And there they are before long in bed sleeping side by side till midday, when they awake, as if the last months had never existed, though feeling a little uneasy with their naked bodies side by side, while supposedly he has no demands – though this is the truth, he doesn't, she belongs to the Egyptian – and supposedly their love comes slowly, exploratively, two dogs of the same breed who sniff each other, eventually barking triumphantly, when they recognize on their breath a common urge, a chemical kinship that's lost in the depths of Darwinian tables. He feels as if she were a part of him, as if he has a part of her inside him – a xenolith, a stone shard embedded in another rock.

The day unfolds in bed with intermissions for food. She gazes at him, photographs him – four poses on the couch in the living-room with his blue T-shirt and shorts – interrogates him with a teasing jealousy. Her steady caress strokes his face, spreading the blood in his veins, relaxing his pores that irregularly follow his frenzied panting. Before leaving, she gives him a look that he'll never forget. How could he ever forget a look that is sad and glad at the same time?

# Yoni

## 97.

*Hi,*

*Thanks for your letter and the phone calls. I'm glad you're so much better [...] As you yourself wrote, the day we spent in Athens was 'moving, tender and brought us even closer together'. It was 'honest and innocent'. You told me that at last I had the opportunity to see you are you really are. Don't forget, in our own, our most intimate moments, whether in Athens or Paros or London, you were always yourself. There, you didn't change, you didn't wear any mask. I think I always recognized that.*

*It seemed silly that we needed a little time to feel comfortable with each other the last time – we had to overcome each other's defences, inhibitions, shyness. I wasn't sure who I was with as, superficially at least, you seemed changed – though deep down inside me I don't think you've changed – something that made me feel under pressure, insecure. I also felt rejection, as before you were so effusive – which I always liked in you – while now you present a cold, controlled self.*

*I now realize how much I learned from our relationship – priceless lessons about life for my future course. I remember the lovely and positive things we shared, our deep communication, the confiding of our secret feelings and fears, our common language, your tenderness, our union in love, your acceptance of my abilities. I hadn't felt that way for a long time. What drove me away was your virulent behaviour. I don't think anyone else would have stood it for so long. It's still a mystery to me what really goes on inside you. You have so many positive attributes yet you seem to scorn them. Life's a marvellous adventure that was given to us so generously. We don't have the right to underrate it so ungratefully.*

*It seems that together we've completed a circle, each of us from a different starting point. And with different motives. Me in order to live, you in order to learn. Last Sunday was waiting for us as always to be together.*

*Love,*

Z.

*P.S. I believe that, like Jane Eyre and Rochester, there'll be light and love at the end, after so much pain, after such tribulation. Life is so very hard and difficult, yet I know that my soul chose it this way. And it chose to get involved in so many experiences in the first three decades of its present adventure. Overly ambitious perhaps . . .*

# 98.

*'. . . The images had been given to me. The whole question was for me to recall them . . .'*

'. . . My life has taken on the shape of the world, it resembles a flat plate carried on the back of six elephants, who in their turn are standing on the back of a giant turtle enveloped by a snake. The snake is coiled backwards and is eating its tail. The elephants are the men, the turtle is the woman and the snake is time. I am a tiny seed sprouting through the back of the shell. Having come to realize my place in this peculiar universe, I maintain my tiny life in that narrow cleft. At times, the back left leg of the last elephant approaches me. There, taking advantage of a skill that I've developed with great toil – I first sensed it on a difficult morning in Lagonissi in 1964 – I'm able to extend a small outgrowth that I've cultivated on my right side – the result of an irregularity in the antibodies on the circumference of the cell, an irregularity that caused a thrombosis in many of my fellows and eventually death. I, however, banking precisely on this dysfunction, this betrayal in the microcosm of the cell, have managed to turn the problem to my advantage, with the result that I'm in a position to touch for an instant, for a split second, the left heel of this elephant when it approaches me, detaching with this specially equipped extremity of mine – a kind of horn-like mixture of proto-cells – a tiny piece of the animal's flesh. Each time that the elephant approaches me, I store up a large amount of its tissue, which I process and so produce the substances that I need in order to change my own composition, in order to metabolize the DNA of the pachyderm, in order that I might gradually be transformed into a replica of an elephant, albeit of minuscule dimensions, able nevertheless to escape eventually from the cleft and circulate freely on the turtle's shell. There, nourished by other seeds, similar to my past constitution, I put my hope in their exponential growth-increase factor, with the aim of eventually attaining the size of the other elephants. Then and only then will I too be able to support my world and have the opportunity that for so many years the other six have repetitively and fatalistically scorned: to tread on the snake with my enormous foot and crush it...'

# 99.

He began working at a steady rate. In effect he changed his profession, entered a particularly competitive field, where he saw things that alarmed him, things he hadn't experienced at first hand, he who'd been innocent enough to believe that in those fields creative co-operation ... and so on. Work for him was a comforting ritual, a daily proof of his existence. So he made sure that his kind of work would be such as to leave traces behind him, objective proof of the time consumed, signs of the passing of each day, of each little end.

He got involved in other fleeting relationships, changing partners of different ages, from different fields. All he managed to do was to confirm his ignorance, the mystery aroused in him by the Other. He went on a few business trips, to London again, to Italy, to Prague. And he at last began to see, to perceive, to enjoy.

And it was then that he felt his soberness being scattered in all directions by the true winds. The winds of reality, those so different from the other wet ones, from those of fantasy. Apparent now in this new clarity, his weight was like a meteor, like a cosmic mass which now had texture, as if you could touch it, feel it, shatter it. He lifted this mysterious mass, this fragment of the universe and he found that it weighed the same as the sum of his organs, the same as his blood, his guts his liver and heart, and after examining it for one last time – why those small craters down on the left, why that greyish yellow amid the dark blue? – he set it up in a prominent, open space. Facing the world. Because the Others stood opposite and embodied him. An endless line, arrayed in front of him, the people, wide open, succeeded each other and waited for him.

'I'll lead myself,' he said, 'thin and persistent for ever.'


## 100.

The seventh elephant.

# Fifth photograph & Zoe

London, 4 December 1996

Hi! I'm writing to you on my birthday, the day before I leave for San Francisco. I'll stay three or four months with friends and I'll visit other States too. I need this trip – you've probably realized that travelling revitalizes me, helps me to sort things out, to start again from the beginning. I think that we needed that going back and forth from one to the other, from your name to my name, from your country to mine – and naturally from the body of one to that of the other.

Now I'm sitting and looking at the photo I took of you the last time we saw each other. You're so different. Of course, I can still make out all your *characteristic features: the need for playing, the posing, the slight perplexity, a little problem with the lens. But you're now something recognizable, an image printed on paper. I was unable to distinguish you in the other photos, you evaded me, as if you were continually coming out of and going back into the photosensitive surface. Now I can see you clearly with your T-shirt and jeans, sitting on the couch in your living-room, where we spent such lovely times, and around you all the objects that seem to me to be so dear to you: your books, the CD player, the paintings, the tiny horse. There's something though that I don't recall: that engraving behind you. You didn't have it when we were together, you must have bought it afterwards. I very much like that turtle encircled by the snake, with the seven elephants standing on it and holding that huge plate. I'm surprised at how, while six of them are unmoving and appear devoted to their painful task, the seventh has the opportunity to stretch its leg threateningly towards the snake. Very symbolic. And then I thought how in my dreams I'd like you to be just such an elephant, to be able to lift the weight of your world, support yourself on a shell base and confront the difficulties you come up against head-on. I hope one day you'll manage it. Take care. I'll write to you from America.*

*Good luck with the new start. With love,*

*Zoe*